GUNKY'S ADVENTURES

In the Land of Must Believe

JIM REUTHER

LifeRich
PUBLISHING

LifeRich Publishing is a registered trademark of The Reader's Digest Association, Inc.

LifeRich Publishing books may be ordered through booksellers or by contacting:

LifeRich Publishing
1663 Liberty Drive
Bloomington, IN 47403
www.liferichpublishing.com
1 (888) 238-8637

ISBN: 978-1-4897-2394-9 (sc)
ISBN: 978-1-4897-2393-2 (hc)
ISBN: 978-1-4897-2395-6 (e)

Library of Congress Control Number: 2019909965

Print information available on the last page.

LifeRich Publishing rev. date: 08/05/2019

Story (Poem) Titles

Afterlife Love Letter and Wish (Stoichiometry)

Gap between happiness and despair is a trifling canyon.
Making life so testy to perhaps contemplate abandon.
Which is why we beseech you to keep your eyes open wide.
To see within and beyond, never forgetting hope is there.
And with each breath joy will be experienced for eternity.

Dearest Gunky:

Happy Anniversary, Sweetheart. Whew, I can't stop crying, but I wanted so much to write this. "Come on, Girl", tell him what your heart and soul dearly yearn for him to know: *I LOVE YOU!* Why am I so upset? Because I know I will not be there to hold you when you read this letter. Sorry, my love, but we knew this day would come. Please don't cry. I am still with you in spirit.

This is our special day, and so were all the other thirty-something other ones. From the night I first met you, I loved you. Now, I could make a funny about being your 2nd choice over Blondie, but I do not want to be funny in this letter as I was in some others (Happy Birthday to me, ha, ha!). I want this one to be as loving and passionate as the English language allows, because my singular message here is to send you my true love. What a pair, raggedy man; what a pair.

Ours was the greatest of love stories. So many memories, from the night we met (you were so cool and sweet, not to mention delightfully sarcastic); to our 1st date (free movie in a lecture hall, how romantic); to our pinning (serenaded by Tools); to our engagement (cameo ring in a pair of warm new knee socks, which I needed); to our wedding (yes, I laughed all the way through); to Son's arrival (when the car went bump in the night); and to Daughter's arrival (when the car went bump again; "I'll never have another kid with you!"). So many wonderful memories to celebrate today. Please do. But here are my favorites, for which I have not thanked you enough.

When I was 1st diagnosed on your birthday, you hugged and kissed me, saying with courage and commitment in your eyes we were in the fight together. On the 2nd and 3rd times when I hemorrhaged, you were so composed. On the 4th, 5th, and 6th times when I puked, bled, or shat all over the place, you quietly cleaned up the mess, hugged and kissed me, and we carried on. When I could not sleep, you gave me back rubs long into the night. I don't know how you managed to take care of me, the kids, and work on so little sleep. But you did, you spook!

But the most wonderful and loving thing you ever did was to ask to see me naked after the multiple surgeries, chemo, and radiation treatments disfigured by body. I was so ashamed about the way I looked and I hid the alien result of being gutted like a deer. Couldn't fool you. You were so caring and courageous to ask, and when I showed you, all I saw was love in your eyes. It was a living me that you wanted to see and hold and all the ugliness did not matter. You can't fake this. You told me you loved my soul. It takes an intrepid man of extraordinary compassion and devotion to do this. But that's you. You were always there, St. Gunky, light of a silhouette.

Now I come to the hard part for me. You are probably alone today, but don't have to be. The kids are our legacy and are beautiful. Take care of and love them. Both told me often how proud they were of you and how you carried-on as Dad throughout my ordeal. You are their hero. They followed your lead of caring, devotion, and love. But now it's time to take care of you.

You must open your heart and learn to laugh, live, and love again. As I asked in my Valentine's Day letter, which I also wrote in advance of this day, please do this for me. No rush. You will find another woman to whom you will say, "You'll do." ☺

Please take care of Elio the Magnificent. I never thanked that silly little stuffed elephant for his humor that helped me cope those dark days and nights. You performed magic together.

Last, thanks for your every-day notes; you found so many ways to tell me you loved me. ***I wish you will continue your writings, especially your poetry.** *They and you are so beautiful and you must share them with the World; thanks, Gunky.*

I hope you find some special way to celebrate today. If you have trouble dealing, I am so sorry, but do not despair. I am free of pain and in a better place now. Be at peace and gentle with yourself. Embrace the joy of life.

Look for a sign, which you might not see right away. That will be me beaming my love to you, which will dry your tears, warm your heart, and comfort your soul.

That's all, Babe. Not light-hearted, but full-hearted; not despair, but joy; no joke; all 100% love. Goodnight, Dad. Take care. Stay safe. Sweet dreams. We'll be together again soon. BCNU. ♥

A few days after the passing of his beloved wife, Gunky discovered her extraordinary letter in a handwritten notebook entitled, "How to Get Along Without Me". Just as his heart was crushing and tears flowing he read her subtitle, "For a Dummy". He had to smile because she always knew how to zing him. The notebook was a simple "How To Guide" for the tasks she had done faithfully for him until the end: finances, laundry; and shopping. She knew he was helpless doing these basic tasks by himself. He would try to carry-on as best he could, as she requested.

With time, one wish resonated from "She who must be obeyed." (Credit John Mortimer). What follows is Gunky's response to Petruskha's challenge to continue his writings. It had been Gunky's Mom who had first challenged him to write poetry after she believed he was becoming too hard of a man because of the dangerous work he did in the early 1990s. Gunky's first poems are included herein under the title of "Xtraordinaire (Silent Sentinels)".

So begins Gunky's Adventures. You are about to embark on 25 journeys, one each for the next letters of the alphabet, done merely for the sake of doing so. These tales, each of which begins with another of his poems or ditty, are not chronological. Some relate back to Gunky's co-author's remarkable letter, notably his reply, "Inspirational Inferno". All of Gunky's stories end with a "wondering".

Proudly, and with no prudery, stories are free of profanity and sex and drugs, but not sarcasm and Rock & Roll. Their genre is intended to be apolitical, so please dare not make it otherwise. If any political incorrectness is remotely fancied in any dialog, appreciate these tales originated in the past, which cannot be changed. Gunky's time machine is currently in the shop.

Above all, please rest assured that no one or no thing was; is intended to be; will or can be harmed by the content of these short stories.

Read on and be amazed and amused, enlightened and inspired, hopefully shedding tears of joy and sorrow along the way. In the end, you Must Believe.

If you are wondering, and his hope is you will 25-times more, "Gunky" was the lovable childhood nickname given to him by his dear Mom for reasons never learned, nor will be. Let's begin.

Beware of Croopers
Busting Hippies
(Doublecross that Bridge)

Walking in from all over the land
Spontaneously to a seminal spot to be.
Tried to join in what was happening,
Was told not the place to be!

"No way, Pop, I'm a college sophomore; kids are not going to stand in hot cow flop just to listen to rock." All Pop ever said in response to Gunky's claim was, "You were 500,000 hippies off!"

This exchange occurred in July 1969, while Gunky was home for the summer to work for Pop and with Older Brother painting houses. Pop would join them at 1 pm after working his 10-hour route as the local milkman. The boys had helped him deliver milk, butter, and eggs through waist-deep snowdrifts uphill both ways during frigid dawns in upstate NY. Every frost-bitten moment was worth it when Pop let them ride bareback blocks of ice bareback across the cooler.

Pop's first job is apropos to this long-hair hippie-freak tale because of the other milkman up North. There were plenty of thirsty villagers to go around for both liquid-nutrition distribution engineers to earn a wage, albeit $65/week, far below the poverty level. One day Pop's milk buddy pulled beside his truck to share a secret. "Two men calling themselves promoters want to rent my cow pasture couple of weeks in August." Giddy as a schoolchild, he chuckled, "It's like stealing."

When this unknowing, soon-to-be crowned business genius told Pop what was planned for his fields both "Didn't get it." Neither did Gunky. So, in late August, when the two lads drove home for lunch both were oblivious to the historic gathering amassing all around them.

"Downtown" in their hamlet consisted of a 4-way intersection. When they tried to drive through slowly, as legally allowed by the blinking yellow light, they were stopped by a tall State Trooper. "Can't go up there; road's closed; turn right." Asking "Why?" got an icy stare. When they said they lived up the hill, the Trooper snarled, "Sure you do; so claims everyone else; now move it!" To their rescue came the solitary local volunteer Constable. "No sir, dem boys do live up there!" The Trooper reluctantly lifted the roadblock, but warned, "Move on now; not the place to be!"

Any need to identify what was a-happening? It was merely "3 Days of Peace & Music" on a dairy farm a few miles north of Gunky's homestead. The concert played-on as-advertised, along with rampant alcohol and drug abuse, not to mention open sex, or as Pop called it, "Piece".

A year later, Gunky returned home with his fiancée to meet his folks. Turns out the upcoming weekend was the 1st-anniversary of Woodstock. "Hey Pop, want to go see what's happening?" Pop's reply was immediate and blunt. "Hell No! Word's out the cops are hankering to get even with the hippies for getting away with everything last year and are going to bust-em all. They're bringing in school buses to herd all the dopers off to jail. Not the place to be!"

Gunky was startled but smart enough to not pursue his idea. Next day, however, Pop dazed and confused Gunky with a surprising change-of-mind. "Hey, let's go see what this hullabaloo is all about; we'll go in your car." "Oh well", Gunky sighed, "Guess it IS the place to be."

So into his Beetle loaded the four of them, his bride-to-be in front and her in-laws-to-be in back. Pop was not kidding. As they approached the main site, there were the bright orange-yellow buses and an army of law enforcement. "Wow, they mean business!" Right then, out of nowhere, a tall State Trooper stepped out in front and ordered sternly, "Out of the car!"

Gunky thought right-off this was way-out-of-line authoritarian, but knew to pick his battles. He almost protested when the Trooper pointed his finger at his parents shouting, "You, too!" After they all got out of the car, he commanded, "Up against the car, face-forward, and spread it!"

Gunky was mortified seeing his fiancée and parents being patted down. With a cold stare, the copper finished his frisking saying, "Now, all of you get back into your car! You, slowly drive up there then around up and drive away slowly. Not the place to be!"

Shaken, Gunky popped the clutch too soon and stalled his psychedelic bug (different color hoods and fenders, kludged to repair damage from hitting a dear). Regaining composure, he restarted, slowly turned around, and calmly proceeded to drive away. Payback is Hell!

"See ya, Pop!" revealed the genius of Gunky's Old Man, who in one fell swoop had just got even for all the shenanigans to which Gunky had ever subjected him.

Seems Pop knew the good Trooper from his milk route. They had schemed over other the last few days how to give Gunky a long-hair hippie-freak surprise.

The Good Trooper then flashed a smile and Peace Sign. Gunky's Mom gleefully exclaimed, "Why, what gentle hands and what fun? I'll never get to do that again!"

Gunky would go on to marry the young coed, who not only got frisked, but also insight into her intended's family. She had many laughs retelling this tale over their 36 years' of marriage until her passing at age 57.

Pop initially pretended to look angry, but then let his short hair down and busted-a-gut laughing.

To everyone's surprise, that hard-core WWII jungle combat vet embraced Woodstock, saying, "All these young kids were trying to do was have fun listening to music outside."

Pop was a firm, but fair, man, ahead of his time and oblivious to the alleged generation gap.

If you are wondering why Gunky minimalizes his brilliant practical jokes (he shares some in later adventures), remember who not only taught him how to pull them off, but also who humbled him.

Never underestimate the Power of the Pop.

Close Encounters of the hooters Kind (Unseen)

Witness a glorious visual trick.
Nature blindfolding, visibly thick.
Out of nowhere dancing wisps appear.
Suspended silent in still crisp air.
Translucent pillows jockey to haze.
To mystify, beautify, dazzle, and daze.
Focus your senses on this joyous event.
Dreamlike scenes meant to circumvent.

This tale has all the makings of a teenage camp-fire tale, haunting Gunky to this day. Dare to imagine being stranded in the dark woods with storms thundering above; thick fog rolling in below; a snake; a sound; and in a cemetery. Promises to be a hoot!

The dog days of summer magnified the malaise manifesting within Gunky's gang, if you can call his 3 buddies that in their small hamlet. Grandma had passed away earlier that spring and it wasn't his turn to burn paper trash from the grocery in the foundation of the demolished hotel. He missed Grandma and the $1.25 per burn, but more importantly, playing with fire, legally!

The lads couldn't continue their Stickball World Seriousness because they had run out of balls. Being the strongest, Gunky had been persuaded by his gang to switch from naturally batting rightly to keep him from driving long balls beyond left field. The ancient graveyard balls rolled into from there had to be haunted. Switch hitting didn't really help because although right field was longer, balls smacked out there would roll into a patch of tall grass in which creeping critters had been seen. G-Gang's Rule, "He who hits dem in der gets dem out."

Gunky was never in a hurry to retrieve his tape-measure homeruns. What he once thought was an old garden hose turned out to be a huge blacksnake. After stepping on it, both vamoosed in opposite directions, never looking back. Gunky took a little off his swing after that encounter. There would be more frightening ones to come. Read on if you dare.

Returning to school in a couple of weeks was looming large that fateful Friday night. Grandma had bought Older Brother and Gunky an AM transistor radio about a year earlier. Gunky was trolling through all the frequencies for anything recognizable, hearing only a lot of static.

However, the bizarre noises he could tune-in over the fringe bands were intriguing and menacing. He was convinced that the eeriest ones were the harbinger of an alien invasion.

Grandma, who grew up on a nearby farm with no electricity, indoor plumbing, or formal education, was entranced by such gizmos. After making a windfall selling her farmland to become the local airport, she vacationed in Florida every winter. She moseyed its beaches collecting artifacts of denizens of the sea, her favorite a large dried-out starfish. She promised it would be Gunky's when she passed, whatever that meant (he still has it). She was also captivated with the nascent US space program and never missed a winter rocket launch.

During her last ever Sunday afternoon chat with Gunky she prophesied, "During my childhood, we rode into town using a horse with a buggy behind (extent of her ribald humor), and now I am watching man trying to fly to the moon. You will see more change in your lifetime than I did in mine." A typical teenager's reply might have been, "Sure, Grandma, more wine?" But Gunky knew better; she was a teetotaler. We know her prophecy came true, but we digress. There is another destination besides the moon beckoning, the dark forest nearby.

Gunky was alone in his bedroom listening to the radio with earphones, all three items he had to share with Older Brother. Seems Older Brother was sharing something else even closer to Gunky's heart that night at that Back-to-School Sock Hop. He sure wished he could make a swap at that moment, a radio in exchange for his dreamy crush!

Preoccupied that they might be dancing together closely, Gunky schemed to stay awake so he would know exactly when Older Brother got home; the later, the more fun they had. As Midnight approached (go figure), Gunky was awakened by something, not sure of what. Gathering his wits, he heard an odd sound for the first of many times. Thinking it came from the radio, he switched it off. But the faint noise continued, sounding like clinking metal, audible even with the radio off and earphones in. Heebie-jeebies kicked in when he pulled out his earphones and the noise seemed to be coming from within the room. His next move was to glance at the door, which he saw closed and locked, thank goodness. His 2ⁿᵈ floor windows were open that hot, still, and humid August night. Facing north and east, the noise entered stereo-like. Ever so slowly, the sound faded away. Fatigued from fright and lateness of night, he nodded off. Sweet dreams were not in store for neither Gunky nor his gang the next couple nights, only fun frights.

Shortly after 1 am, Gunky woke in a cold sweat. He was dreaming that something really bad was about to happen. Sitting up, he realized the clinking had returned and was now louder. Heart pounding, he looked under his bed without getting out, slipped, and fell to the floor. Regaining his senses, he squirmed on his belly to the nearest window. Peering out, he realized the noise was coming from the nearby forest up the sandy hill past the tall grass, in "Badland".

Fascinated by trees during solitary nocturnal hikes among them, Gunky was spellbound. He thought he knew all the sounds out there. "What goes bump in the night and sounds metallic-like?" Summoning his courage, he put on a shirt, shorts, and sneaks and silently slunk downstairs out to the back stoop. His was careful not to wake his parents, even though both could sleep through a thunderstorm. All the way down and out the sound called to him. There would be more creepy callings to come.

His quest began by sneaking over a dew-drenched right field, stopping just before the tall grass. "Wonder if Mr. Garden Hose is asleep?" The allure was unbearable so he sprinted through the tall grass with feet barely touching the ground. He lived!

Gunky's terror amped when he realized the worst had just happened; all had gone silent. "Yikes, it knows I'm here!" Instantly, he crouched and waited for something to happen next, holding his breath for what he'd claim was 10 minutes (in actuality, 10 seconds). Just when his pulse and breathing slowed, they were jolted back up to abnormal. The sound had moved and now came from the edge of the woods up the sandy hill just ahead. "What do I do next?" he asked, and then oddly answered to himself out loud, "Be a cat!" With the gate and curiosity worthy of a slinking feline, he climbed on all-fours up the dirt mound he imagined was Everest-like.

Halfway up it happened again, silence; not even katydids! Deciding cat-walking was silly, he stood up to see better from where the sound last came. After standing perfectly still for another eternity (all of 30 seconds), he briefly considered abandoning his quest. The next adrenalin rush came when he thought he heard the sound again. So faint, he wasn't sure if he were hallucinating or if some thing were clinking. If he were hearing it again, there was an even bigger problem; the invisible noise maker had moved again, and without a sound. Gulp!

Surprisingly, knowing It had moved didn't frighten him. In fact, it had a calming effect, because it offered a measure of inevitability. So he bravely continued climbing the hill upright.

Getting closer seemed to be the brave thing to do. Whoa! Just when the tinkling became loud and clear, he had the next jolt. This return from quick quiet was accompanied by a bright flash 20 yards dead ahead. Bursts of light usually don't end in silence. Gunky knew this was really bad.

Initially frozen in place, Gunky found himself tumbling down the sand bank head-over-heels. Seems his first stride in retreat was not down the hill, but outward, horizontally! Just as in classic cartoons, he seemed temporarily suspended in midair until gravity resumed its pull. Anyone witnessing to this aerobatic feat would have surely wet their pants laughing. But for Gunky, there was certainly no humor, and only a little pee.

Gunky hit the ground running as if Beelzebub himself were in hot pursuit. Arms and legs pumped like pistons so fast he landed on the porch in a blink. Exhilarated, he quickly and quietly crawled upstairs to his room, locked the door, and hid under the bed. His "Tell Tale Heart" thumping, he crashed into a deep sleep, failing to realize two things. First, he had just negotiated Mr. Snake's Home twice and had survived. Second, Older Brother was snoring soundly under the covers of the double bed above. For now, just store away these details because of more immediate importance is the disturbance.

After wolfing down breakfast Saturday morning, "He Who Stole My Woman" asked Mom and Pop if he and broken-hearted could be excused. Just before he had slipped a note under the table asking Gunky to meet him on the stoop in 10 minutes, sharp. "He's going to kiss and tell!" Older

Brother had appeared preoccupied at breakfast, not unnoticed by Pop, who kidded that he must have had a lot of fun because he had gotten home so late. Gunky did not like hearing this at all. When Gunky went upstairs to their room to dress, he discovered the radio had been left turned-on all night and now its batteries were dead. Buying batteries was a big deal because it was up to the two brothers to pay for them. He again missed getting the $1.25 burn money. Ah, paying for new batteries must be the topic of our urgent porch rendezvous!

Older Brother was waiting on the glider and began talking quietly as soon as Gunky was within earshot. "I'm freaked out. Heard a weirdo sound at 1 am last night walking myself home from the dance. I think Russians have landed in the woods." Forgetting about batteries and babes, even after learning Older Brother had walked home alone, Gunky confirmed he'd heard it, too. Gunky then recounted the details of his mini-reconnoiter, not mentioning anything about pee.

Gunky then realized he must have locked Older Brother out of the room and asked how he had gotten in. Older Brother said he didn't remember, as he was frightened out of his wits. Having a younger brother's pride, Gunky didn't mention he was so scared he slept under the bed. Older Brother whispered, "Let's assemble our commandos and conduct a night raid; don't tell Pop."

So cool was Older Brother thought Gunky. His reference to the suspected identity of the intruder was apropos given the time period during which this eerie tale was unfolding. It was during the height of the Cold War.

Not a year earlier, Older Brother and Gunky hid under their bed because of another sound from the sky. Then, it was the drone of high-altitude prop-engines. So remote was the area in which they lived, neither could resist watching and listening to every plane that ever flew overhead, albeit few and far-between. That terrifying night both thought for sure they were heavy Soviet bombers from Cuba, where nuclear missiles had just been parked. This made sense because there was a US airbase nearby. They're coming to nuke us!

Older Brother comforted Gunky, "Commie radar can't see us under our bed." This was the same Older Brother who told the G-Gang our parents acted as flying monkeys in the Wizard of Oz.

At breakfast following that harrowing night, it was Pop who was on the front porch talking, but not to buddies, but vigilantes. The debate was over why he had refused to build a bomb shelter for his family. "Don't you love your wife and kids?"

Gunky's Old Man had only a 3rd-grade education, forced to drop out of school at age 10 to find work for food for his family during the Great Depression. He was also a 3-year combat vet, fighting in Southeast Asian jungles during "The Big One".

Fatefully, he got the nuclear physics correct in his rebuttal. "Ain't going to hide in a cellar like damned rats if them evil Reds attack. Shelters won't help. When the sirens wail, we're going to park our asses in lawn chairs in our front yard; watch the biggest, baddest, brightest fireworks display of all time; and kiss our and your fried butts goodbye. See you all in Heaven, only a little sooner!" Well said! But, we digress again; why fear Soviets when you should fear something slinking about in a haunted forest?

Inserting playing cards in-between spokes with clothes pins, the duo saddled their beefy, clunky 1-speed pseudo-motorbikes and roared off to gather their cohorts. Unfortunately, their pals had to join in family events that day and were not available until after dinner. Disappointed, but not daunted, they agreed to rendezvous in deep right field just after sunset when it was cooler. Each also knew it would be scarier then. Late that afternoon, the aftereffects of an intense pop-up thunderstorm, a "cracker", as Gram called them, made sure of this, laying down waist-high, ground-hugging fog. Darkness seemed to take forever to arrive. Enhanced by a New Moon, foreboding didn't get any more wicked than that way came.

Teenage boys will be...you got it. A once semi-serious expedition to find a noisemaker derailed into hijinks. The first was the length of black garden hose purposely laid in the tall grass. Gunky didn't find it a bit funny, but let them have their laugh, planning his revenge. This stunt would be the inspiration for the subplot in later Gunky adventure, "Go Lightly".

Upon arrival at forest's edge, they tried riding a fallen tree, but slipped off because of its slimy wet moss coating and silliness. Not hearing any strange peep out of anything for 30 minutes, Older Brother suggested they venture deeper into the wood. Volunteers all. Tramping noisily through the thick brush in the fog at night was fun, but they soon felt like right fools when they realized they should have kept quiet so as to not spook the spook.

One antic had everlasting consequences. It started with Gunky discretely lagging behind; sneaking around ahead; hiding; then jumping into view with a screech. "Hide-and-Boo" was always a hoot, especially when enhanced by darkness and haze. But it would be Older Brother who would give everyone super-duty chocolate swirls. To no one's surprise, he disappeared next. Copycat! The lads searched high and low in the thick underbrush only to find no trace of him. The stunt quickly turned from fun-to-frustration. "Come on; come out; cut the crap!" Still nothing. All at once, he nonchalantly reappeared yards from where they had just searched. Older Brother was so cool; he simply vanished and unvarnished! His antics secured him as Gunky's hero and would be the inspiration for another tale, this one involving "Invisibility".

Ah, did we forget something? As if scripted, the very moment "Sneak-and-Scare" ended, the sound returned. Now it was in front of and above them. Shocked backed into reality, all screamed and ran smack into each other. "That hurt!"

Older Brother then took command over the chaos, "Chill, we out number it!" But as soon as all caught their collective breaths, it changed its overhead position from just ahead to just behind them. Scram!

Pop was standing on the front porch when Older Brother and Gunky arrived gasping for air. He casually asked both what they had been up to (as if he didn't know.). As Pop's wry smile hinted, they were not to be believed when both simultaneously said, "Nothing."

It was Mom Gunky who then surprised all when she suggested the boys gather their friends and check out the buzz coming from the fallen satellite in the woods. "What?" She said, "It's the talk of the town." She had overheard this rumor at the grocery store while buying birdseed there.

For a split second Gunky thought, "$1.25." He almost blurted out it wasn't a crashed Sputnik, because they knew it could move silently treetop-to-treetop. But Older Brother subtly kicked him first, stealthily putting his index finger to mouth whispering, "Not here; not now."

The last weekend nights before school brought no joy. Everyone now knew about "The Sound". It lost its intrigue when adults became interested. Despite these downers, the idea of using a tape recorder restored their enthusiasm. They all agreed they finally had something important to record. It was another wonderful gift from Grandma Gadget.

Shortly before departure, Older Brother muttered a couple of his same-age buddies might be tagging along, Charlie and Dave. "Gee, don't they hate each other?" Older Brother then asked if the gang still wanted to go forward. Why? Grimacing he said, "Ha! Because Dave's crazy!"

After arrival at the deepest edge of right field, Gunky let Older Brother walk through the tall grass first. After all, he thought, "He's tastier." Dave was waiting on the far side. When the G-Gang near where he was standing, he menacingly announced, "I brought along a friend who wants to give that annoying noise a piece of its mind."

With that, Dave brandished the hunting rifle he had been hiding behind his back. The gang was stunned, fascinated, and troubled all at once. Suddenly, Dave became visibly agitated. He had just caught sight of Charley arriving near home plate and asked, "Who invited him?" Seems Dave owed Charlie money for a long time that he still did not have.

Without warning, Dave leveled the rifle to his shoulder, aimed it at the approaching Charlie, and squeezed off a single shot. Charley dropped face first, the sight of which punched all breath out of the gang's lungs. Dave coolly blew the smoke from the muzzle saying, "Creep had it coming."

As if that weren't shock enough, Charlie jumped up and ran away. Dave then callously mumbled, "Wasted a good blank." Older Brother had underestimated Dave's insanity. All knew it wasn't a setup between Dave and Charlie to scare G-gang members straight. Sheer madness.

Dave went on to become an attorney in Canada. Charley never spoke to the gang again. A few years later he would be shot and killed his first day in Vietnam. Sucked to be Charlie.

The G-Gang stood still in silence for a hard 5 minutes, after which Dave got bored and started walking home. No one tried to stop him. As soon as he was out of sight, the sound returned loud and clear, this time not from the woods ahead but from the cemetery past left field. "Do we dare?" With the aspect of summer ending and school beginning, all hustled toward the burial ground to sneak up on the perpetrator. Who are you calling crazy now?

All this time the temperature had been cooling. Coupled with high humidity, a thick ground fog billowed in around the four brave lads. What a sight, tombstones smothered in marshmallows!

At first, they crouched behind a family of old stone markers to plan their attack. When they stood to split up and surround the sound, a succession of loud cracks and brilliant streaks flew over them through the mist 10 feet above the tombstones. "Duck!" It was Dave, funning himself firing tracers into the night sky. Nuts would not be too harsh a word for him now. Pleading "Cease fire!", the gang hit the ground. Each learned what dirt tasted like that night.

Hearing no more gunfire, they fled the cemetery, sprinting to respective homes where each was greeted by concerned parents, who had also heard the shots. Some serious splainin to do.

Telling Pop it was Dave caused grave concern. He knew Dave's Old Man and went to have words with him. That whole family would leave town a month later for up North. Pop ordered Older Brother and Gunky to discontinue their sorties into the forest. That was probably the only time they ever did what Pop asked them to do the first time asked.

Rumor had it a bounty had been put on the "Thing in the Trees", which would have been higher if it actually had been Reds. Later that night, an armed mob assembled near the tall grass. Gunky was cheering for the real Mr. Garden Hose to be awake and hungry.

Sadly, the sound was heard nevermore (Thanks, Edgar).

Next day, Gunky went to the local library to look up what might have made such a sound. Other than the woods and the fire pit, the local library was where he most often spent his free time. Walking in under the pair of stuffed ravens gave him a clue. "Because it was in the trees and moved silently top-to-top, wouldn't a prime suspect be some sort of bird?" Not a bad logical deduction for a 13-year old sleuth, heh?

Knowing the library well, he searched on his own and found a trustworthy book on birds, a copy of which he would buy later with some of his burn money and cherish forever. About 15 minutes before closing, an white-bearded, elderly librarian walked from his office and quietly placed another book beside the gem Gunky had been enjoying all afternoon. This book was ancient, musty, and wrapped in brown paper with no markings except for a 4-digit hand-written number on its spine. A red ribbon marked a certain page. Voila! There's the answer! "On rare occasions, baby owls may make a sound like clanging metal." Gunky yelped in delight, which did not disturb because no other patrons were in the library. Hearing the antique Grandfather Clock chime five, he went to return both books. The old librarian was nowhere to be found, so he left both books on his desk with a note in pencil, "Thank you, kind sir!"

Solving this summertime mystery was delightful, but deflating. Gunky wanted this adventure to last forever. With a slight tear in his eye, he put his hands in his pockets and started walking home. Their emptiness reminded him he had to buy batteries. The path to the store required him to walk past the same Town Hall where the dance had been held an eternity of nights before. His thoughts juggled between batteries-to-a buck twenty five-to-babes.

Done. The terrorizing tale of a close encounter is all tidied up now, right? Not quite; you may have noted a couple of loose ends. If so, you are correct. Perhaps there will be more!

First, what on Earth caused the flash? Next sunshine-filled day, Gunky returned to the spot from where he was certain it had beamed. Mr. Snake must have been on holiday.

After careful searching, he jumped for joy when he found a piece of broken glass the size of a egg amongst the sparse, spindly brush. One would think he had just found the Hope Diamond.

Lying down on his back with his head where the glass had rested, he looked out and got a glimpse of a plausible source of light, a car driving down through waving trees on the opposing hill. At night, headlights could beam through to the exact spot where his head was lying. If the trees swayed in the breeze just at that moment, headlights might shine onto the glass for a split second. This made logical sense to Gunky, who was just then beginning to read Sherlock Holmes. Mystery #1 solved by a Junior Sleuth nicknamed Gunky.

Second, where in the woods had Older Brother been hiding? All now can be revealed; maybe.

Gunky knew where because he had found Older Brother, who winked urging he pretend he hadn't seen him. Gunky, a quick study, played along, never mentioning his discovery to the other members of the gang. He honored this conspiracy between blood brothers.

Are we done? Not quite. After all, this is a story about close encounters of the hooters kind.

Late that afternoon, Gunky convinced his gang to join him at the scene of the flash; see the evidence; and flaunt his detective skills. When they got to the spot where his piece of glass had laid, however, it was not there. "Ah, did you lose your pet shard? Hey, let's put out an All-Points Bulletin for a fugitive sliver of terror!"

Gunky got miffed and before he could think, accused the lot of coming to this spot ahead of time to steal the evidence. To his surprise, they all plead guilty, saying it was a stunt well worth their while after seeing the stupefied look on Gunky's face. Gunky then burst their bubbles by claiming this could not be true because he had not told anyone of finding the glass, only the flash! Now it was the gang's turn to have stupefied faces. All's fair amongst G-Gang members.

Older Brother compounded the situation by revealing yet another conspiracy, not about hiding glass, but about hiding himself. He boasted everyone had seen him during their searches through the bushes. For grins and giggles, he winked at each, silently asking each to not reveal his location to the rest of the gang. "Pretty neat trick, huh?" Stupefaction returned when each search party member revealed where they had recalled seeing Older Brother.

None reported the same spot, and no spot matched where Older Brother claimed he had been hiding all along. All swore they were telling nothing but the truth. All's unfair amongst G-Gang members.

To this day, no one knows for sure "Who was zooming whom?" with regard to the elusive hideaway or phantom crystal. What happens within the G-Gang stays within the G-Gang.

Gunky grew up (questionable), moving on to other adventures chronicled next. One sunshiny summer day home from college to visit Mom and Pop, he stopped into his dear old library to reminisce. He was met by the same pair of birds over the entrance.

After an elderly librarian introduced herself, he recited his boyhood adventure and how helpful the bearded old librarian had been in finding the hand-numbered, brown-paper-wrapped bird book that solved the mystery of the hoot owl.

She then dropped a couple of her own non-nuclear bombs. Are you ready?

First, she testified that long before this avian (librarian speak) adventure, every book originally been covered in brown paper and numbered consecutively had been unwrapped and tagged with a typed Dewy Decimal label. No book would have been otherwise by the time of his adventure. Not convinced, Gunky quizzed how she could she be so certain. Her direct reply, "I was in-charge of this arduous task and personally made sure that every last book was upgraded. I even got a certificate and a bonus for doing so."

Still not satisfied, Gunky suggested that perhaps the librarian who had helped him was still alive and around and might shed some light on this mystery. In a gentle gesture intended to be convincing, the kind lady librarian rested her hand on Gunky's. Her eyes twinkled when she leaned close to Gunky and whispered, "Why dear, there has never been a male librarian at this library; all of my lady coworkers can attest to this."

If you are wondering if Gunky is still experiencing mysterious close encounters, a little birdie may hover by and let you know.

Do a falling Gunky Land on his feet? (Meow!)

Who has 9 lives and a nickname so neat?
Who always lands upon his own 2 feet?
Who never had a broken bone to fix?
One cool cat, call-sign Felix.

"Wow, I can go to varsity games for free as an 8th-grader if I wash balls? Deal, Coach!" The tools of Gunky's 2nd-ever paying job consisted of a basin, scrub brush, gritty soap, elbow grease, and dirty practice basketballs. Really wasn't hard work and he was keen of the minty smell of the soap. What was really neat was how differently the balls looked, sounded, and felt after washing. Their metamorphosis was from brown-to-orange; thud-to-squeak; and slick-to-so sticky that even Gunky could palm a ball with one hand. Dunking time!

Two years later, Gunky had planned on continuing to play junior varsity basketball, then cheer on Older Brother playing varsity. For some dastardly reason, the Coach moved Gunky up to varsity and made him compete for the guard position Older Brother played. Mean!

Both had played friendlies against each other for years in their back yard; each knew the other's moves cold. Their never-ending games nearly always ended tied. Gunky's heart was not into trying to bench Older Brother, especially his senior year; he had earned his starting spot.

As they sometimes do, the situation sorted itself out. Older Brother broke his ankle the last practice before the season started and Gunky replaced him by default. Older Broker was always on the bench to cheer, and then critique, his every play. Gunky's varsity team would win only 1 game in each of the next 3 seasons, which, ironically, decided the league championship by upsetting the 1st-place team at the time. Even a blind squirrel…

This fateful off-season episode was initiated one Sunday morning by Older Brother, a massive pro-football fan. Frustrated by poor TV reception at Gram's house (only TV within miles), he conspired with Gunky. "Coach is not in his cabin in the Pine Grove this weekend. Why don't we go hotwire his antenna to our TV so we can watch the big game?"

Gunky quickly volunteered to do the high work. With Pop's best extension ladder and tools, the duo hiked 100 yards through 2-feet deep snow to the quaint cottage where Coach lived. They assumed he was not home because his hot wheels seemed nowhere in sight. They jacked-up the ladder to the tall pine tree onto which his antenna was mounted. As Gunky was climbing up, Older Brother whispered, "What was that?" Both stopped and listened. Must be the wind.

Gunky continued his climb and was about to splice the cable when he felt as if he were being watched. Looking over the roof he caught the first glimpse of the green convertible. Startled, he glanced down to see a 5-foot man in shorts, sandals, and sun glasses holding a double-barrel at his hip. "Going to count to three; 1…" Gunky recalls how cushioning and cold the snow bank was underneath and how fast Older Brother ran…away, but not hearing "2". Looking up on his back, he was now alone among the falling snowflakes and temporarily deaf.

Now what's a Gunky going to do? He picked up the long and short remnants of the ladder and lugged them back to the garage. He then went into the kitchen, which was dark. Mom slowly walked in and said she was woken up from her nap by what she thought was a backfire.

Gunky's pale face was incriminating. "It was Coach. Shot-gunned the bottom off of Pop's ladder." Surprisingly, after hearing about such an act of violence, Mom was remarkably calm. "Is that all?" She knew there was more to the story. "No. I was on the ladder when he shot." Again, her composure was eerie. She knew Gunky was at fault for having put the ladder up on Coach's property, but certainly didn't condone what he did.

Nor did she want to confront a "mad man with hair trigger", who had already shot at someone. "Show me the damage."

Gunky took Mom into the garage. "Pop will be upset if he finds out. Get the saw and we'll cut the bottom ends off square and rub mud on them to cover the fresh wood. He won't see or need his favorite ladder for months." With dispatch, cuts were made and mud smeared.

To this day Gunky never confirmed whether Pop (who passed away of natural causes at age 83 after smoking at least a pack of unfiltered cigarettes a day for about 70 years) ever found out about Mother-Son Conspiracy. Gunky made sure to volunteer to do all the high work when painting houses for Pop that following summer, especially when the long-ladder was needed, which was covertly 3-feet shorter.

As for Coach, about a year later, he was sentenced to a very long cabin, ah prison stay for driving 95 in a school zone with the top down and drunk, then committing another hit-and-run.

If you are wondering what the ratings were for Gunky's full-butt landing, back in the days of the Soviet Union, Summer Olympic gymnastics judges would have scored it (out of 6.0): 5.6; 5.2; 5.8, and from the Russian judge, 12.6 (sardonic Cold War humor).

Ever Rising (Daily Gift)

Pause in cool darkness quietly still.
For glorious curtain riser to remove the chill.
Elevating with an ever-brightening glow.
Black-to-gold floating upward slow.
Nature's distant spatial daffodil.
Silently delivers its spectacular thrill.
Do not fear, it will not forget.
See it rise to see it set.
Never failing.

This story was launched with a win; carried-on with a coffee, and ended even.

When World War II erupted, the US began drafting some of its finest by lottery. This would be the one and only one Gunky's Old Man would ever win one. Such a big deal, a photo of his getting out of bed groggy-eyed with the winning ticket in-hand graced the front page of the local newspaper. Ah, for at least that short period of time, everyone seemed to know his name.

Celebrity, as we know, has its quirks. Three weeks later, after not getting any orders, he strolled down to the local draft board to find out what was up. His was greeted by a chorus of, "You're still here?" His reply, "Yep, I'm not mad at anyone yet!" He soon would be.

Next day he was on a train to Army boot camp. For 2 years thereafter, he endured hard-core survival mode in the jungles of the Asiatic Pacific Campaign. Life there was dominated by a 75% Rule: Nearly-complete a landing strip; take cover watching it get strafed; and do over." He made Sergeant twice. Second time was after differing with a superior officer about his taking better care of transmissions in the motor pool because they were more valuable than a soldier (7¢/each). Dental work was required, not his, worth more than a nickel and two pennies.

Circumstances were much more atrocious than this. Only words he ever quietly shared were, "Surprise attack!"; "They shot at ME!" and "Ended it with my bulldozer blade." Gunky's Older Brother keeps the few black-and-white photos of gruesome kamikaze attacks. Yes, war is ugly.

He returned home a hard man, softening upon marrying the love of his life. The second love of his life would be born later that year. Tragically, he would receive a life-altering phone call weeks' ahead of the expected date. Upon arrival at hospital, he was told his wife had died in childbirth and his son was close to death with little hope. He was lost soul

To add to his stress, no newborn with his namesake appeared to be registered. Checking the list for times-of-birth, they found a mystery name. When they got to that baby boy's room, the priest who had given the dying mother her last rights explained he had blessed and named the weakening baby after himself for the pending death certificate.

In shock, Gunky's Old Man was given the standard, but in this case, serendipitously, fateful, advice, "Go to the cafeteria for a coffee." As he entered the elevator he noticed its only occupant, a young woman, appearing pale and wobbly. As the elevator descended, her eyes rolled up and she fainted. His attempt to catch her before hitting the floor failed. Help arrived as soon as the elevator door opened directly in front of the hospital coffee shop.

After regaining consciousness, the young woman explained to Pop Gunky that she hadn't eaten all day while trying to watch her weight. She had been advised to go to the café after donating some of her rare blood to help a young mother stay alive during a premature childbirth.

After coffee and sandwiches (barely touched), she shared with Pop that she was a beautician at the hospital mortuary and had donated her special blood before, but never had fainted.

She then asked Pop what had brought him to the hospital, which was answered by silence.

After a deep sigh, he replied, "Thank you" and she immediately knew what.

She then expressed sorrow for his loss but joy for his new addition. She knew this gritty widower would have a difficult time taking care of a baby and promised to check-in to see both when she could. She would like to offer some guidance before the young Lad and his novice Dad were allowed home. She kept her promise and soon thereafter a loving relationship blossomed.

Many of you readers may have already guessed the identity of this woman. Well done! Eighteen months after meeting, they were married and she would become the mother who would nickname her first child "Gunky".

After 45 years together, Mom Gunky would pass at age 67. Dad Gunky would never quite be the same.

Over the next 4 years, Pop and Gunky shared many memories, some recounted herein. A minor one remains a mystery. It involves why listeners would always chuckle after Pop would joke, "Two are cold, but three are frozen." Unfortunately, neither Older (Half) Brother nor Gunky ever learned why this punchline was so amusing. Both still laugh when hearing it anyway.

One memory most relevant is a postscript to the event that began this tale. As Pop approached retirement, it became evident there was a glitch with his receiving Veterans' benefits. After investigation, Older Brother and Gunky learned that in the rush to process his papers, after putting them aside for the press, his last name had been misspelled. For all intents and purposes, he did not exist in WWII. Because records had been bombed, burned, and/or buried, this situation was understandable (hard prayers here for the MIA). Pop was never bitter, but did once whisper, "There are a few enemy dead who knew I was there; 32458058." Enough said.

Working with local their congressman, partial records were recovered and needed benefits granted and much appreciated. The box of medals was ignored. As keepsakes, Older Brother and Gunky each took one of Pop's Army Air Corps dog tags with their namesake misspelled. This jinx would be passed on to Gunky, for after he scored a touchdown or hit a homerun, newspapers would list him as Bunky, Lunky, or Tunky (but never Funky, Hunky, or Junky). However, when he made an error that lost a baseball game, Gunky. Made his Mom so proud.

In his last year, Pop shared some singular words-of-wisdom with his #2 Son. "Saw you won a PhD; heard it's the highest-earned degree. I only got to the 3rd-grade. But I did learn something from life you should realize:

You can't argue logic with an idiot." This advice was adopted by Gunky, as will be demonstrated in later tales.

In the days before he passed, this special man of 83 shared the gift he had received from decades of driving 3rd-shift roach coaches and milk-delivery vans. "I got to see every sunrise for over 50-years." Better not bet he could not describe each and every one. Glorious.

If you are wondering how Gunky remembers Pop, he cherishes a fond reminder he's given by every morning, which signals Pop will always be above to illuminate his way. Golden!

flicking is Dangerous to a Career (not Cool to be not?)

Come on Gunky light my fire.
Try to ignite some science desire.
Not the time to wallow in the ire.
So what's the name of the new hire?

Gunky was rarely allowed to speak about what he did for living because of its nature and the danger of copycats. This was upsetting because he really wanted to make students aware of all possible career choices, especially his unique one. So it came as a great surprise one day when his manager asked if he wanted to be a Science Ambassador and speak at an Invention Convention. Didn't take Gunky long to say, "Yes", even after learning he had to use his own vacation time to perform the weekday afternoon gig.

Driving to the local high school, Gunky practiced out loud the points he wanted to make to the young audience, understood to be small group of select science majors. He thought hard to think of a catchy intro. If he didn't capture their attention quickly, he might be labeled as just another nerd and the experience a waste everyone's time. Need a great opening line!

He got to the administrative office 20 minutes early, where he was met by the Vice Principal, very appreciative of his willingness to speak promoting science. She told him the audience was slightly over 600, almost the entire high school. Realizing his challenge just went from difficult-to-nearly impossible, Gunky muttered to himself, "Oh well, the more, the merrier, right?"

After being introduced as having a PhD and receiving a lukewarm welcome, Gunky took center court on the gymnasium floor. He stared into the packed bleachers for about 15 seconds, just smiling. By their varsity jackets he knew the back row was filled with jocks, whose attention he needed to get early and sustain. "And now for the hook."

"Good morning everyone. You just learned I'm a doctor. Bet you're all wondering what type? What, you ask, there's more than one type? Yes! You've all heard of medical doctors; they have people as patients. You've all also heard of veterinarians; they have animals as patients. Well, I'm a third type of doctor. And I have my patient in my pocket."

What Gunky did next would get him accused of high crime at this school. All he did was reach into his pocket, pull out a lighter, and flick it.

"This is my patient, fire! I've spent most of my career trying to understand the awe and mystery of how this inferno comes alive; stays alive on its own; and how it can be snuffed out. Fire intrigues all of us. I decided at an early age to study it seriously. Want to perform magic? Hold a spoon over the tip of the flame like this and you instantly turn an invisible gas into a black powder. See this, it's called soot. No scientist on this planet knows exactly how a flame makes so much soot so fast. It's one of the hottest, ah coolest mysteries in chemistry and physics!"

To say his intro was captivating would be an understatement. Gunky grabbed their attention, including the jocks in the back row. He told them how combustion heated their cozy library; cooked their yummy barfeteria food; and fueled their hot rods. They listened keenly to his tales of travels around the World and beyond fighting fires in pipelines, supertankers, and spacecraft. "I did so safely and smartly, and never have been burned because I like me."

As he was selling science, he couldn't help but notice a suit offstage looking mean as Hell (pun intended). "Whoa, is that dude is peeved at someone! Wait, he's glaring at me!" Gunky ended his presentation by asking, "Isn't science cool?" and got not only a standing-O, but also an immediate order, "I'm the Principal; come with me to my office at once!"

Gunky was confused. He entered first, followed by the Principal, who slammed the door behind. "What the Hell did you think you were doing?" Gunky admitted, without guilt, "Why, trying to give an engaging talk to students as to why studying science is neat."

His reprimand, "Well, you weren't supposed to break strict school policy. We work very hard here to enforce our no-smoking policy and you had the nerve not only to bring in a cigarette lighter but also light it! I've never seen such insubordination! What's your manger's name and phone number? I'm filing a complaint!"

His diatribe was interrupted when a woman came to his door, which he opened, glanced out and then screamed at Gunky, "You'll be hearing from me!" He looked at Gunky then the door; Gunky got the message. During his drive back to work, Gunky didn't mutter a word (usually talks to himself). On arrival, his manager was waiting in his office. "What did you do this time?"

Gunky matter-of-factly told him what he said and did, to which his manager replied, "Congratulations, you just got the Principal suspended for 1 day without pay. Seems his Superintendent not only heard your talk and was wowed, but also heard the admonishment and was miffed. A letter of apology will be sent to you by tomorrow. Thanks for conducting yourself so professionally. Now get back to work; your smoking break is over, ha!"

All Gunky said to himself driving home that night was, "Well, I'll be damned. I'm going to keep that lighter as a souvenir! Flicked only once."

If you are wondering if Gunky ever played with matches when growing up, yes, setting a short-lived mini-forest fire at the age of 12, which might be why he would never be able to run for President? Never going to hear "Hail to the Gunky".

Go Lightly (Transvection)

Inhale lifting, exhale drifting
Relaxing the body whole.
Suspend thinking, ignore blinking
Releasing your Earth-bound soul.
Eyes wide open, staring down
Hovering weightless all around.
Tranquil, timeless, quiet, calm.
Steeped within a gentle balm.

After learning Gunky had solved a mystery of Sherlock-Holmes' caliber, one of his superiors bemoaned, "Why, that was only marginally above mediocre."

Gunky might have ignored this undiagnosed creativity envy had not his singular solution been recognized as "first-of-its-kind". Gunky's patent award escalated "Snob Master's" condescension, "That's rather lightweight in creativity from my view!"

Because of his self-declaration as being ever more learned, "Brainiac" felt obliged to deliver vilification in as highbrow manner as he could by sneering down a stuck-up nose. To enlightened associates, his scholarly elitism was specious and easy to see through. Oblivious to how he was ill-perceived by others, he consummated his self-appointment as "Mastermind" by espousing, "I see the bar for ingenuity was set rather low on that one!"

Such blatant belittling really jazzed up Gunky. His "Haughty Heckler" will be referred to hereafter by ever more flattering aka's. However, instead

of maintaining his composure, Gunky lowered his dignity, dishonoring
this *cause intellectuel* by glowering, "I'll never try to have another patentable
idea again!"

Throwing a tantrum only turned the recurring mockery into ridicule.
Don't fret etymologists; this "Low-Class Antagonist" wouldn't know the
difference between these two words even if one existed. Although Gunky
conjured up many brilliant ideas over the years, few were patentable. As
most inventors know, Step-1 is innovation; Step-2 is being first. Visionaries
know being creative also involves proper timing; imagine that?

When Gunky's patent boycott persisted, and free money from their
licensing fees ceased being dumped into his coffer, "High-Maintenance
Man" mused, "Are you just not trying or have your creative juices dried
up?" Gunky tried, to no avail, to plead his case that, "The fluids are still
flowing, but they're running a distant second."

What is worse than one of your bosses not making a decision? It was
"Big-Idea Man" commanding, "Send Gunky to Creativity School, at
once!"

Before his 3-day sentence, ah seminar began to learn the path to
enlightened thinking, pure pouting pursued. "What could anyone ever
learn from such bogus, phony-baloney nonsense?" Gunky insisted that
all these adjectives be used for emphasis. The "Clown Prince of Creating
Creativity" then ordered Gunky to, "Shut up and take the class."

So visible was Gunky's torment that even "Elitist Man" saw it, who
boasted to anyone who would listen, "That'll learn him, smart ass!"

So deeply upset he had revealed his innermost contempt, especially to
a foe that would cherish knowing, Gunky, head down, glumly marched
to his cell, ah classroom. Only a half-hour into the ultimate three 8-hours
days, he was already to blow a head gasket. But then out of the corner of
his eye Gunky spied a smirk. Instantly his spirits rose as he had a first
glimpse of a possible escape plan. "Wait, because this class is all about
expanding one's horizons, why not have some fun at the expense of "You-
Know-Who Man"?"

Committing to *cause creativite*, Gunky winked at "Mocking Man" and
then scribed a battle cry in the virtual cloud floating over his head, "OK,
I'll take you up on your challenge, dumb ass!"

Opening questions from the "Creativity Gurus" to baseline the
sentenced, ah students seemed benign enough. "What are your favorite
animal and color?"

"What in Heaven above could answers to these lofty questions ever reveal about my level of creativity?" STOP! Gunky closed his eyes, took a deep breath, and recommitted to his quest. "Now that I am beginning to see what's really up, let's play along."

"Tinky Winky" evoked riotous laughter. "And just whooo is Tinky Winky?" questioned "Disdainful Man". "Why, a colorful imaginary creature with an inverted triangle on its head; TV screen on its belly; and red purse in its paw." Disgustedly, "Leery Man" drawled, "OOOKKKK?" The banner now being sky-written over Gunky head read loud-and-clear, "Head's up!"

Gunky's response to part two unleashed even more guffaws from "Color-Blind Man". "Why, Tinky Winky's color, of course", said matter-of-factly. An irate "Really?" shot back from "Unknowing Man". Confidently, Gunky pleaded, "But purple is the logical extension to Answer #1." Public rebuking by "Maniacal Man" persisted, "This is a class in creativity, NOT logic." Gunky reminded himself to stay aloof to such facetious ridicule and take the high road in all attempts to him put down. Almost respectfully, Gunky coyly whispered to himself, "As you will soon see!"

Little did anyone know what creative evil lurked deep in the mind of Gunky. "Now is the time to not be grounded."

After deliberately provoking this Q & A skirmish as a trial balloon, Gunky decided to get a leg up on his planned uprising. Unbelievable to even the despots, ah dons, he was a model student, participating in every exercise with no visible rebellion aforethought. He kept a low profile because the "Imagination Police" were suspicious, looking for any opportunity to bring him down. He buried his thoughts of insurrection below ground. "Now you see me; later you won't!"

Ever more over-the-top taunting could not lower his resolve. One high hurdle involved, "What is the most visual color of marker with which to write on a white board?" After Gunky printed in black, he was verbally minimalized as to why he had not chosen purple, "Out of homage to Tinky Winky" He explained he picked black because it could be seen better by his fellow captives, ah colleagues in the back of the room. "I'm-Above-All-You Man" then derided Gunky, "You are just not elevating your level of creativity! Black may be logical, but purple is not only just as visible as black, but also has flair."

Gunky acquiesced (sort of) by making chartreuse his signature color. Darkly, he thought, "Flair this!"

Late on Day #1, the "Custodian of Cleverness" announced the format of the test that would determine if a student were worthy of a Creativity School Certificate. The final exam would be a 3-minute speech on any activity the prey, ah presenter either wished to do (high marks) or had done (lower marks). The only rule was that the performance demonstrate clearly the ability to use imagination to develop an original idea.

Out of another corner of his eye, Gunky noticed "I've-the-Upper-Hand Man's" leer was now more confidently displayed. This vision uplifted Gunky's spirit so much he allowed himself a smile, but only on the inside. In "Manager Speak" (puke), Gunky vowed to "Ideate a robust high-level strategic paradigm." In "Gunky Speak", this translated into, "Up, up, and away!"

All Day #2, Gunky hummed to himself the ditty of the Scarecrow in the Wizard of Oz. Indeed, he did have one, and was about to show how cunningly subversive it could be used for a higher cause. Gunky could barely restrain his giddiness, becoming light-headed at the mere thought of winning such a lofty prize as a Diploma in High Creativity!

"Insecure Man" was now watching over Gunky more closely than ever. At times, he suspected Gunky was a touch detached from Earth. He tried his saddest best to learn covertly what was up in his head. Some interventions had a hint of cleverness, but all were telegraphed. Gunky deliberately faked preoccupation to nurture "Easy-to-Fool Man's" imaginings. "Man, do I really want to goof-up your head."

Gunky did, at times, become detached. His mind was not always in that cellblock, ah classroom. Once it wondered back to his college freshman dorm room, where he had an epiphany from with a flashback, "Water Wars"! His room was across the hall from two 1st-rate jubilant, ah juvenile delinquents with a passion for water fights using balloons, buckets, and even the emergency fire hose. So addicted were they to aquatic vandalism the clothes dryers in the basement broke down from excessive use. A repairman could have retired in that dorm!

Given their proximity of his room, Gunky was a frequent drowning victim, intended or not. So tired of getting soaked that the next time his head came up for air he protested to the water bombers as behaving too rude, crude, and aqueous, ah abusive. Their attacks lacked finesse, denying victims any opportunity to defend other than wearing a wet suit. Much to Gunky's surprise, his reprimand was challenged, "Wet's up, Doc?"

"Water Thrown-Downs" were declared for the next 2 weeks. Their singular goal was to get an opponent's dorm-room floor wet. The method had to rely on cleverness, not just random acts of deluge. Other inmates, ah inhabitants, in the dorm would be Judges. They were solely responsible for monitoring setups, which required opponents' rooms being accessible to challengers, but for not longer than 10 minutes. They would ultimately decide, "Wet or Dry?"

First to douse the opponent's room floor after equal attempts would be baptized "Raining Champion". All cheered when the Dorm Director proclaimed, "Gentlemen, start your wetting!"

Gunky returned from class a few days later to find his door ajar and difficult to open. Suspecting an ambush (duh), he stopped pushing. Everyone else already knew ahead of time about this first gauntlet and were standing by watching in galoshes. With abject apologies to the Kingston Trio and Tom Dooley, they badly sang, "Hang down your head soggy Gunky, poor boy's floor ain't gonna stay dry."

After assessing the situation, Gunky surprised all by saying, "Let's go to dinner." Permitting his opponents food, however, was not his intent. By jazzing Gunky all through their junk food feast, they were, in actuality, providing him with subtle clues about the device they had erected on his door. They boasted it was impossible to dismantle. Putting all their hints together, Gunky knew more about it after dinner than before. The water was in a bucket strapped to the door knob such that it would tilt and spill if the door opened further. Looked like a classic setup. Gunky was respectful, but failed to shutter when his opponents taunted him by saying "We're mechanical-engineering majors."

Gunky's first move was to hijack a mirror, shower curtains and rods, and towels from the communal bathroom. Returning to outside his room, he slid the mirror through the partially open door to see what the threat looked like, and, most importantly, which way the bucket would tilt. Seeing it would tip to the right, he constructed a makeshift frame as a catch basin using the curtain rods and towels. He then practiced sliding the contraption under the next-room's door to the approximate landing zone of the spill. All this time his opponents shouted, "Dive-Dive-Dive!"

Gunky then took a deep breath, slid in the barrier, then carefully but firmly pushed on the door. Voila! The bucket tilted and slowly poured water onto the tarp where the towels soaked it all up. Nary a drop hit the bedroom floor. He then carefully slid the wet blanket out from under the door and into the hall, where the "Arbiters Aqua" declared, "1-Dry (Love)."

Needless to say his opponents claimed foul, the basis for which was their device had not been defeated because it did pour water onto Gunky's floor. The judiciary took great pleasure reminding these "Wet Losers" that, "The official rule states the floor must get wet." No one was drowned in the close-quarter combat that broke out next. A good wet time was had by all.

It didn't take long for Gunky's opponents to exploit his tactics. They covered their bedroom floor near the door with a thin premade catch basin. On seeing it, Gunky pretended to be riled, which was deceitful. His real motive was to get extra time in their room for a better pre-inspection before he put his plan into action. They just let a shark into their wading pool!

The judges were disappointed when Gunky finished installing his aqua bomb. All he appeared to do was carry an empty bucket into their room; look at the inside of the door; go into their bathroom; and then return to balance a now water-laden bucket on the top of a half-open door in plain sight. They had failed to notice the pipe wrench tapped to the inside of his leg under his pants and how long it took him to fill the bucket in their bathroom. "That's it?" to which Gunky replied, "I tried; perhaps it's better to just let them swim, ah win."

Before the judges could convince Gunky this was suicide by drowning, his opponents arrived at their now booby-trapped door. Gunky conceded, "Did my best, so let's get this over with." Just when his opponents began celebrating, Gunky suggested, "Victory dinner anyone?" With much jubilation they replied, "Sure, but first let's take down your dumb bucket." They did so with ease with nary a drop hitting their bedroom floor. They then rushed into their bathroom where they poured the water down the sink. Splash-splash, cause-cause; Oh! What a dowsing it was!

Students claim water-curdling screams echo in that dorm hallway to this day. Turns out Gunky had removed the drainpipe from under their bathroom sink. Water dumped down it flowed straight onto his antagonists' bathroom floor and to their bedroom floor and under the tarp. All Gunky said with a dry smile was, "Game, set, and splash!"

"Wake up!" Gunky almost blew it, because he was not responding to another question from one of his inquisitors, ah instructors.

After answering on which color of sticky paper it was best to write notes ("Why, fluorescent lime green, of course."), he resumed his sea-voyage reminiscing. He would use that experience as a template to strategize another endgame. Vu déjà.

When forced again to momentarily pay attention to the tripe, ah teaching, he heard the singing of a Van Halen tune in his happy head, "I get up and nothing gets me down."

All at once he achieved enlightenment. His plan would be to deliver as high a dose of altitude silliness, ah sickness, as possible to "Condescending Man". Jump!

When "On-a-High-Horse Man" saw Gunky temporarily detached from reality he resorted to some awful taunts, all too inane to record. Although Gunky dreamed wickedly acerbic counters, all went unspoken. Their deliverance would surely have exposed his planned trickery. He denied himself, faithfully sticking to his flight, ah game plan, a "higher level of creativity".

The last 6 hours of "How-to-Become-an-Instant Innovator" were nothing short of an excruciating load of "ineffable twaddle" (thank you, Dr. Watson). Gunky endured the pain by scheming up a plot twist to add to his finale's sensational uplifting performance. Although his planned parlor trick would be presented to the entire asylum, ah audience, it would target only one person. Just when you thought it safe to order me to creativity class, "Look up and see me if you can!"

His launch began late the afternoon of Day #3. Because he had participated so faithfully (not surprised?), Gunky was given the opportunity to be the first prisoner, ah presenter. Sometimes, remembered Gunky, giving thanks, you have to be lucky as well as prepared. This is it; you only have one shot, so do him, ah, up right!

After sincerely (he was) thanking his torturers, ah teachers for the past 20 hours of edumacation, Gunky announced his life's triumphal accomplishment was not a dream but a reality. Summoning all his best public-speaking skills, Gunky passionately told the class what his audience thought was an allegedly fake tall tale.

Seems almost 20 years earlier, because of job-related stress, caused, in part, by managers like "Clueless Man", he had mastered a relaxation technique based on deep breathing. Gunky invited all, especially the now "Puzzled Man", to join a class participation.

Everyone was asked to chant, "There is a place, a quiet place, where you can go to find peace and tranquility; breathe in, breathe out; breathe in, breathe out; you can go there now."

Lemmings! In less than a New Yawk minute, all, including "Oblivious Man", floated away! Gunky's next two premeditated words dropped the bottom from under this level of tranquility. Everyone but one was now grasping with astonished laughter. All Gunky asserted, calmly, clearly, and most genuinely, was that whenever he relaxed using this method, "I levitate."

Gunky was told afterwards by his cellmates, ah classmates, that his facial reaction to this outburst was a mixture of bewilderment and hurt feelings. In a timid, begging-for-acceptance tone, Gunky pleaded, "But, it's true."

Not unexpectedly, there were few converts. Most thought they were at comedy club and had just heard a very well-timed punchline. As Gunky watched his sincere reply drift slightly over their heads, he whispered ever so softly to himself, "Fools, now prepare to fall!"

Gunky sought empathy by admitting he was spooked the first time he lifted off, discounting the class's reaction to the nervous laughter typically accompanying surprise. All he succeeded in doing was tickling their funny bones more. "Obnoxious Man" hissed, "Hey, Joker, why don't you hit the road with your comedy shtick?" Little did "Talent-Scout Man" realize, "How prophetic?"

Gunky made one last-ditch attempt to end this purposely initiated circus by boasting he was a "Master Levitator". He proclaimed proudly that while hovering, he also slowly rotated, giving a panoramic view over all horizons. All this pretension did was to bring down the house again. The new tune humming within Gunky's head was, "Off I go into the wild-blue yonder."

With eyes wide open, Gunky guardedly scanned the audience. Out of the last corner of his eye, he witnessed exactly what he had intended and hoped would happen. Yes! The skeptic who laughed the loudest was, indeed, "Unimaginative Man", who was now rising from his chair most agitatedly to say something. Wonder what his question will be? NOT!

With vengeance aforethought, he first commanded, "Silence in the room!" Then, in as a smart-alecky a tone as he could muster, quizzed, "Now that you've conquered levitation Dr. Gunky, what could you possibly ever do to top your achievement?"

With both feet firmly planted on the floor, Gunky looked directly into "Be-Careful-What-You-Ask-For Man's" glaring eyes and professed, as he had planned to do the last 2 days, "invisibility".

Gunky didn't bother looking back as he buoyantly bounced from the podium straight out the door past the stack of diplomas. He heard the standing ovation from his levitating, ah rising, new friends and felt the cursed heat beaming from the eyes of a now "Red-Faced Man", who protested using words Gunky had begged to hear and will forever cherish, "That is NOT funny!"

Within 30 minutes, Gunky was dragged in for interrogation by his immediate supervisor. "What the Heaven you did you just do this time. I want a straight up answer!"

Gunky admitted, without remorse, "Why, I just gave 'I'll-Teach-You-How-to-Instantly-Become-Creative Man' a lesson in imagination." Not for a moment did his boss believe that, "All I was trying to do was to pass a course I had been ordered to take to upgrade my enlightenment." To which his boss replied, "Then you admit you tried to get a rise out of him?" Gunky's plea was delivered with cool confidence and humble honesty, "Guilty, as charged."

This post-class inquisition had also been anticipated. Before sentence could be passed, Gunky put his foot down, as preplanned, "All creativity aside, top levitation and invisibility if you can!"

The message was received loud-and-clear; the pun apparently not. Stammering, his boss demanded Gunky do to what he had claimed he could do, "Get invisible, NOW!"

For an instant, however, Gunky, stood defiantly unmoved in full view. His dark side had dreamed up some one-liners specifically tailored for just this moment, which he now unleashed.

The first was a polite, "'Foot-in-Mouth Man' should be ashamed and offer ME an apology, because it was he who cannot tell the difference between comedy and creativity!"

The second was even more polite, "'Imposter-of-Imagination' wouldn't know creativity if it flew up his bum and bit him."

Gunky said neither. He knew his command performance would stand-up forevermore in the "Creativity Hall of Shame, ah Fame". Instead, he requested, "Permission to get back to my three days' backlog of work?" After all, Gunky, being of sound body and mind, does levitate.

Didn't take long for his exploits to "go viral", an expression not yet invented, without the benefit of today's social media. Next day, Gunky got more high-fives and respect-inspired backslaps than he ever imagined. Although he and his stunt became legendary, he modestly declined the offer to become the "Poster Child for Creativity" saying, "I'm over 50 years old!"

There were the copycats who tried to top his feat. The attempt earning highest marks occurred when Gunky walked past a group of good friends. Initially, their eyes tracked his on a horizontal level. A few paces later, they glanced gradually upward to a higher plateau and then downward back to horizontal. Uplifting, but fell flat!

Other wannabes needed a bit more creativity. Instead of pretending to see Gunky levitate while walking, they made believe they didn't notice him at all as he strolled by. Nice try, but Gunky exposed the obvious glitch in their masquerade. They remained silent after he said "Hello" to each by name. "Hey people! I'm invisible, not mute!"

When they acquiesced he was still audible, Gunky awarded their valiant attempt by proclaiming, "Your grade will be "Ah", with the "h" neither invisible nor silent."

With time (a few years), his arch enema, ah enemy during that classic 3-day "Battle-of-Wits between One-Armed Opponent", became a dear friend. "Contrite Man" admitted sincerely to Gunky that he had never been so deftly set up in his life, and that he deserved the fall. "Kudos to you, joke was on me." As proof, the now "Humble Man" proudly presented Gunky with the diploma he never received, marked with an "A+", written creatively in purple.

When it comes right down to it, both had passed Creativity School that day. Gunky went onward and upward to win more patents, selling licenses and bringing new riches to a now more "Appreciative Man". At his funeral, Gunky knew he had just levitated to Heaven.

If you are wondering if Gunky still wanders the Earth searching for new ideas, he does, albeit sometimes ever so slightly above it.

Hide Your Impotent Papers, Please (No Peeking)

When someone curious rummages through your stuff.
Whatta ya gonna do? Circle slasher!
When someone assiduously spies on your stuff.
Whatta ya gonna do? Ambusher!
Gunky ain't afraid of no snoop!

Curiosity kills cats; sometimes humans with a similar affliction get immunity from prosecution.

One lunch, Gunky joked with colleagues that one occupation he really wouldn't mind having would be as janitor. He would then have a free run of the place and imagined that after finishing his daily work as fast as possible, he'd use the balance of his shift to browse the library. His purpose would be to soak up science while not bothering anyone else's affairs. The response from his friends was instant, "Really? Aren't you doing this now?" Gunky admitted, "Touché!"

There would be a hiatus before Gunky would kid about his fantasy again. The day he resumed was memorable because of the seriousness of someone else's preoccupation. His colleagues swore him to secrecy before revealing what had been going on. Gunky promised never to tell another soul. If you wish to help Gunky keep his promise, stop reading now, heh, heh!

Seems another colleague shared a variation of Gunky's vision. But instead of browsing the library, he was snooping through everyone else's offices! One of the admins arrived early one morning only to find him standing by her desk reading the papers on it. After awkwardly claiming, "I was just looking for the papers I gave you yesterday", he simply walked away. Problem was she couldn't remember if he had given her any papers, so she did not report him.

About two months later, another admin experienced a similar encountered. This time, however, there was no reason for her to have had any of his papers, so she reported him. She never heard what happened as a result of his intrusion because Human Resources told her it was "Strictly Private". Feeling aggrieved, she felt obligated to tell her colleagues *sub rosa* for their personal safety. This was how and when Gunky came in the know.

Being extraordinarily busy, Gunky just ignored this drama. "So the guy's nosy, big deal." Gunky soon had a change of mind when…you guessed it.

Gunky sat down at his desk one morning and had the feeling something wasn't quite right. What he suspected was some papers on his desk seemed to have been shuffled.

His reaction was to set a trap by arranging papers on his desk and memorizing their positions. He tried doing this late one long day, but concluded it was simply too much effort. Next day, guess what had happened again? Yep, but this time Gunky was certain someone had riffled his papers. This 2nd violation was a call-to-action. "Who ya gonna call?"

First thing Gunky did was to go through the company's monthly newsletters to find a photo of the suspect. Eureka! Next, he went to the library to find a newspaper advertisement for the movie "Ghost Busters". Why you ask? First, Gunky was not sure if the slash in the red circle went from the upper left-to-lower right or from upper right-to-lower left. No, Gunky wasn't dyslexic; he just didn't remember! Second, he had to go to the library because the Internet hadn't yet been invented yet! Gee, how did we ever get along before cyberspace? Quite well!

Next, he taped the photo to the center of an 8½-by-11 inch white piece of paper and correctly drew a circle and slash around and through it with red marker. Last step was the master stroke. He flipped over the paper and with red-inked rubber stamp, printed "Strictly Private" (justice!). He placed this enticing document on top of his desk out in the open. Game, set, and trap!

Gunky knew that in a court-of-law he never could have proven beyond reasonable doubt if his office had been intruded the next day, let alone by whom. Suffice it to say, the circumstantial evidence was compelling because his voyeuristic colleague did not speak to him for the next 6 months! Further temptation and problems were eliminated shortly thereafter when all papers were required to be filed in locked cabinets and all doors locked overnight.

If you are wondering if Gunky knows what you are up to, fear his red-rubber stamp; it is mightier than the cat.

Inspirational Inferno
(Why Candles are Lit)

Eternal is our curiosity
Of your spiritual luminosity.
You shine and sparkle; Oh! What a thrill!
As colorful and lively as a daffodil.
You frolic and flare, shimmer and sway.
Mysterious, transient, while trying to say
That with each wisp of bright golden blaze
Hope will flash from gloom's dark haze.
Your beam makes it clear when despair is near
And melancholy darkens our head.
Watch and believe and your mind will relieve
With joy and illumination instead.

On our 36th Thanksgiving as husband and wife, after our dear kids left our cozy condo, we shared a poignant moment staring into each other's eyes. We both knew. Something wasn't right. After all, we had 10 years' experience with this curse. This time, however, something was different, unlike anything before and we did not want to believe it. After all, the CT scan on Halloween showed the tumors in her liver and lungs were static. Nothing, absolutely nothing, appealed to her taste, not even her blessed staple, strawberry sherbet. The only thing she wanted was more breakthrough pain meds, which she rarely used. Not even my back rubs throughout the long night gave her the comfort for which she thanked me sweetly. This night, they were not working and she was just trying to make me feel good. We both knew of her fate, which went unspoken.

When the pain would not stop and the vomiting began, we went on autopilot and repeated what we had been done many times, take her and her pre-packed bags to the ER. She said she was worried about some monthly bills having to be paid and packed our checkbook in her green and white-striped beach bag. That's Mom for you, to the end.

Arriving at hospital, our respite from home many days and nights, I asked if she wanted a ride in a wheelchair. For the only time, she said, "Yes." I knew she did this for me, so I couldn't see her beautiful eyes as we went in.

The only, repeat only, time I ever saw fear in those eyes throughout her courageous battle was after a CT scan when the doctor would give the readings on her breast, lungs, liver, and spine, but not mention her brain. She would then ask. She told me one dark night she could and would not deal with the curse spreading to her head. She said she would be selfish for the first, last, and only time, and not fight. The battle would be over

During our stroll inside, I flashbacked to all the surgeries, radiation, and chemo, then shuttered and thought, "She's really in trouble now." Never once did I think this might be the last time.

Although the doctors and nurses bless them all, tried to be miracle workers, the ER experience was a nightmare. When the morphine she asked for kicked in, she began hallucinating and her mind left this World. No, not her mind, her lovely, clever, and witty mind. It would take me hours to coax her to drink enough contrast so she could get another CT scan. It broke my heart, whatever fragments remained, when her head cleared for just a moment during this ordeal and she said, "Don't ever leave me." She knew I would always be there. I will never know for sure how much comfort it gave her, but after her lips became caked and chapped, I wiped them with a moist towel and applied lip balm from her purse. It certainly made me feel better.

At about 9:30 am, a pastor, with whom she had worked at Hospice, came to see us as he had faithfully done every hospital stay. He mentioned she was doing better, but that today, after she was discharged, she would need much more care at home. He said he would begin to make some arrangements. He was a saint whom we dearly loved and respected.

At about 3:30 pm, the oncology doctor came to see us. Because her practicing oncologist was on Holiday, she was on-call this Thanksgiving.

Ironically, it was she who first told us of the curse in her breast on my birthday a decade earlier. She asked me to step outside. In the 7N hallway, with those beautiful hand drawings on the ceiling and extraordinary candor and compassion, she whispered, "It has spread to her head; she will not be leaving this hospital." She then asked ever so dearly, "Do you know what this means?" I was numb, but the love we shared allowed me to focus. "Yes." I closed my eyes and prayed, "Dear Lord, take her now."

A year earlier, on a dark night of projectile vomiting after liver, lung, and spine were cursed, I asked, "I am big boy who can handle it. Tell me straight, what are we up against this time?"

Her eyes were as beautiful as ever but sad when she replied, "Two-year death sentence; we need to make plans."

So together, we went through 24 years of memories in our dear, but multi-level home, fixed it up, sold it, bought a one-floor condo, and moved. Throughout this time, her health and strength returned remarkably, and she was happy to do much of the work. She made us new home. She said the move was as much for me as it was for her. I did not want to hear this, but did.

What this last numbing, not unexpected, news obligated me to do was tell her straight that her worst fear was realized. How do you tell your soul mate the worst news she never wanted to hear?

The greatest gift a husband can ever give his wife besides love is truth. I did what she had instructed me to do. Her beautiful eyes showed acceptance and love in return.

About 5:30 pm, she began to have difficulty breathing. About 6 pm, she looked at me and held out her hand for me to help her up out of bed, just as she had done before to take a pee. This time, however, when she got upright she put her arms around my neck. As her weakened legs struggled underneath to keep herself upright, I realized she was not going to the bathroom, but was trying to hug me. It would be my last dance with my rock-n'-roll girlfriend.

As I helped her back into bed, she looked at me and said, "I want to go home." I kissed her and replied, "You are going home." If ever I needed proof she loved me, which I never did, this hug was it. It will always be the most remarkable moment ever experienced. Hours of tears to write this.

At about 7:30 pm, in a matter-of-fact manner, the floor emergency doctor took me aside and said, "She will not last the night. What are your intentions?" I took a deep breath and replied, "DNR, do not resuscitate."

Again, on another dark night months before, she told me that when this time came, I would say these words. Because it was her wish, I would obey if I truly loved her. It was done. I found the strength to do so in my heart.

I called their kids, who got by her bedside about 8 pm. I then held my beloved wife's hands, watched, and waited. Her breathing slowly became labored and irregular.

The nurse on-call that night was an angel. Her compassion for my wife, kids, and me was deeply touching. I felt my beloved's life end through her tiny hands, which cooled, warmed, and relaxed. At 9:44 pm, her beautiful hazel eyes opened one last time, looked straight into mine, and she was gone.

In the end, I am convinced that she was in charge; she made the call. She knew the odds were against her and what she needed to do. She decided to rest-in-peace after only 57 years. It was glorious. She was now at Home.

Thirty-six years of loving, laughing and living together as husband and wife. "To love and to cherish; to have and to hold; for better or for worse; in sickness and in health; until death do us part".

I knew this woman well and of her courage, dignity, grace, and willpower. She would leave me 39 years to the day we first met.
Damn, I loved and love that woman. BCNU. ❤

Petruskha by dearly beloved father and mother
Tricka by dearest father and mother-in-law
Terry by college girlfriends, "sweet young things"
TMR by the computer, post-its, notes, and scribbles
T by her many soccer friends around the globe
Ma Theresa by hospice nurse coworkers
Mom by her loving son and daughter
She Who Must Be Obeyed sometimes
My Immortal by husband, Gunky

If you are wondering, Mom sends signs of her everlasting love to us day or night in the form of a tiny bright spot, her one headlight.

Jinx Come in Threes?
(Three Leafer)

A-B-C-D-E-F-Gs
Does bad news really come in 3s?
H-I-J-K-L-M-N-O-Zzz.
Good news trumps when you believe.

Gunky had but one aspiration in high school. Perhaps it was his harrowing ride in an open-cockpit biplane? Perhaps the yellowed black-and-white photos Grandma showed him of the barnstormer on her farm? Perhaps it was a stirring hymn? All three experiences would put the love of flying into Gunky's blood early.

Not getting a snug fit, Buddy gave up saying, "Straps aren't needed anyhow." Might have been OK if communication between the front and back seats had been clearer. When Buddy shouted, "Wanta do a barrel roll?" all Gunky heard was, "We're on a roll!" and shouted, "Yes!"

Upside down with his head jutting out just above the windscreen, Gunky thought he was going to eat corn from the crops less than 100 feet below. While struggling madly to pull himself lower into his seat, he spied the bridge over the approaching narrows. He didn't think Buddy was loony enough to fly under it. Gunky didn't know how to swim and was relieved when that bridge-storming was completed without contact. The dead-stick landing just-for-kicks was the charmer. Whew, returned to Earth hungry, dry, and alive!

These events would inspire the high-school junior in high school to take the national standard entry exam. Offering little challenge, Gunky scored very high. The physical test also was no challenge, although he had no idea why pilots had to exceed at climbing ropes and heaving medicine balls. Scoring high qualified him for a Senate sponsorship. Weeks after taking the 3rd-exam, the medical, Gunky rode his bike up the long steep hill from the Original Teeny-Tiny post office every day, being fit, in less than 2-minutes. When the letter finally arrive he ripped it open and gasped. At dinner that night, Pop knew something was wrong and said, clairvoyantly, "You washed out." As usual, Pop was correct. Seems excessive refractive error was politically correct in those days for saying "wear glasses". Gunky was offered appointments to West Point and Annapolis, but not the Air Force Academy. Pop recommended "No" to the Army because Vietnam was raging and "No" to the Navy because, as you will recall, Gunky didn't know how to swim.

Unfortunately, a decision was indirectly made for him later that evening when over the radio the Gunky Clan heard his NY Senate sponsor had just been assassinated in LA. It was 1968, and RFK's death caused Pop to mutter a classic and ever-so poignant statement-of-the-obvious, "Guess you're not going to a service academy now."

Gunky, then a senior, had not applied to any colleges because of the early promise of his flying at Colorado Springs. A fallback position had not been planned, but if you graduated high school in NY, you would be accepted to one of its State University campuses.

Older Brother came to his rescue. "Apply to my college where you can earn a BS in chemistry in 3 years, then transfer to a 2nd university and earn a BS in chemical engineering after 2 more; 2 degrees in 5 years." Gunky applied and easily got accepted into this ambitious program.

The next 3 years he would indistinguish himself by earning an underwhelming 2.65 GPA, finishing last in his chemistry class. Seems he enjoyed partying and sports too much. He still qualified for transfer because the minimum entry GPA was only 2.50. His chosen career path was thwarted again, this time by a financial default cancelling the transfer program. Although he had completed all the hard courses for a BA in chemistry and physics, he hadn't completed enough soft courses to graduate unless he stayed 3 semesters more. In those days, you were considered slow if it took you more than 4 years to graduate. My, how times have changed.

What a difference that 9th semester made! One afternoon then Gunky almost did not go to a non-required seminar. Instead, he did and within 15 minutes knew what he wanted to do next, "Go Boom!" The speaker captured his mind and spirit talking about combustion, flames, fires, and explosions. The sole purpose of that Professor's seminar had been to recruit a single graduate student to mentor. The nut had just found the blind squirrel!

Despite tough competition, and to the surprise of many, Gunky won the scholarship. He breezed through the qualifying and comprehensive exams at record pace to become the first PhD candidate in his class. He was ecstatic to work in a lab where he was researching better means by which to snuff out fires using dry powders. Wicked cool!

Gunky will always assert that this advisor was the singular person who taught him almost everything research-wise he ever learned, most importantly, poise under pressure and recovery.

Perhaps the best example of the last occurred the day his advisor and he were working to bring to back-to-life a discarded, but free, analytical instrument.

Gunky had completed all the hardware repairs and was admiring his advisor, a self-taught glass blower, working on the intricate tubing that twisted up, down, sideways, and back again. After several aborted attempts, he finally got the labyrinth finished and tried fitting it into the device. He did get it stuck in, but very tightly and slightly cockeyed. When Gunky leaned in for a closer look, his safety glasses very gently nicked it. Spray of shards!

Gunky fully expected to get yelled at for wrecking in a millisecond the glass sculpture his advisor had so tediously worked on for over 3 hours. Much to his astonishment, "Glad that happened before we had this beast full of toxic combustion gases." He then proceeded to blow another, much sturdier fixture in only 30 minutes that fit perfectly. He never said another word. The moral of this story is that immediately after any crisis occurs don't even try to say, "Oh, snap!" Instead, focus your full attention and mind on recovering. Life lesson learned.

One Thursday in late January his advisor told Gunky to refill the ink in dried-up recorder pen while he went on his lunchtime bird-watching walk. They would try to extinguish a test fire on his return. He never did, dying of a massive heart attack at age 53 just outside. Deep sadness.

Over the next month, equipment would be "borrowed" from his lab; a co-researcher attempt to take credit for his ideas; and he would be told his PhD dissertation could be written up, but only as a Master's thesis. This trifecta justified Gunky's cursing in public for the first time. "Damn!"

After the fog and rage settled, Gunky realized his deceased mentor had freakily suggested a recovery plan. A month before he passed, on the first fateful Thursday, Gunky was reading a magazine that posted jobs, as he was within 3 months of defending his PhD. His advisor walked in on him and kidded him as to why he was reading the jobs section. "You're not done yet."

Gunky asked his advisor if he knew anything about one ad. It was an offer for a PhD graduate assistantship at a major university to study how to make bright light from chemistry. His advisor read it over Gunky's shoulder. "Gee, I know this Professor; he's a good guy. And look, he's paying 3-times the stipend I'm paying you!" Gunky nicknamed his advisor that day, "Clair".

Gunky eventually recalled the chat with his late advisor about the ad. He looked for his copy of the magazine and not finding it, went lab-to-lab to see if anyone else had one. Because all had been discarded, he executed his 3rd option and took the long walk to the main library in the snow. Finding the magazine in the magnificent library was easy, because Gunky had its combustion science section memorized, QD 516.

Trying to make a photocopy was "thrice" challenging. The machine on the 1st-floor was jammed and that on the 2rd-floor out of toner. He then couldn't find a working pen to write down the phone number and the lead in the only pencil he could find was broken, with no sharpener in sight. Once able to write, he almost quit because the application deadline had long passed. Frustrated, he got busy writing his MS Masterpiece. But then...2nd thoughts?

After practicing what to say on a 3rd memorable Thursday, he summoned the courage to call, but the line was busy. The 3rd attempt went through and the voice on the other end said, "Hello, how can I help you?" Gunky hesitated, then replied, "Hi, I know the deadline has passed, but I'm interested in your graduate assistantship and wanted to know if...." He was interrupted by a hearty laugh, "Why, Professor has reviewed 30+ applications so far and hasn't found anyone acceptable. Who did you say you were?" After a deep breath, Gunky said, "Well, I didn't say, but I was the student studying with the late Professor..." Another interruption.

"There you are! My Professor was wondering whatever happened to you. He'd be delighted to talk with you so I'll go get him." Before Gunky could mutter a word he heard her put down the phone. After about 3 minutes, she said, "He's not in. Please give me your number and I will have him call you."

His call came about 3 hours later. Short version (Ha!), Gunky went to that university and made blinding light from chemistry, winning a PhD in 3 years. He did so by working from 6 am-to-midnight almost every day. His motivation? Didn't want to go to a 3rd college to win a PhD.

Before he could finish, there was another encounter that would redirect his career plans. One day, he and 3 fellow graduate colleagues were waiting in class for their delightfully distinguished and eccentric British Professor. He was late, as usual, and when he arrived threw his notebook down in front of Gunky. "I'm leaving in an hour and will return in 3 weeks. Mr. Gunky will teach the class." He left, never saying why.

The four of them stared at each other for a moment when "The Greek" stood. "Professor knows shite about flame dynamics. Mr. Gunky knows all. He will teach us and we will become geniuses." Then he sat down. Because graduate school is basically self-study, Gunky lead the class and all learned a lot about how flames fly fast and why. This Professor never came back, accepting an endowed chair at the University to which he gone to interview. Job opening.

You guess what happened next? Because he had graduated from that university, Gunky had to interview every one of the many deans over 3 weeks to compete for the open professorship. Whew! His answer as to "Why should we hire you?" was, "I'm already taught one of his courses!" He won the faculty appointment over (you guessed it) 3 other candidates. Now what?

The problem Gunky had was he never planned on a career in academics. He had already received 2 other job offers, one each from a small and large R&D company. Too many options!

When decision day came, Petruskha and Gunky decided to place the 3 offers on their makeshift coffee table (boards over a wooden fruit crate). Each was to then close their eyes and put their hand on the letter they wanted to accept. Petruskha went first. When gunky put his hand on top of hers, their university adventure began. A tale onto itself; not here, not now.

If you are wondering if Gunky believes if jinx come in 3s, re-read this adventure. Jinx come in equal-opportunity installments; so do blessings.

Keep an Eye on that Cute Blond (Of the Beholder)

Pretty, witty, and full of spice.
You'll never see peepers so nice.
Five foot two, eyes of blue.
Never know, do you?

She was in Gunky's high-school class and a real knockout, a description soon to be more ironic than you can imagine. Not only cute, she was well above average in intelligence; sweetly satirical; spunky; and a rebel with many causes. Her unconventionality was not contrived. She was a really cool teenage girl with two of the most-strikingly beautiful blue eyes.

When it came to interacting with the 11 boys in their senior class of 18, she did seem to favor one. He was ordinary in looks; quiet in manners; and non-athletic in build. Because he was foreign, he was behind in his schoolwork and 1 year older than everyone else. He would have easily blended into the background if not for his girl friend. They didn't really date but hung around a lot together. One could say she was "seeing" him.

She and Gunky always had fun when together, enjoying each other's company. They sang in a talent show quintet covering folk songs from the 1960s. There never really was any hint of romance; that was, however, until their Driver's Education (DE) class together last semester of senior year. It all started in the back seat; just kidding; well almost.

The first flicker sparked over frozen lake, where the DE Instructor (DEI) had taken them that fateful Thursday to practice driving on ice, a skill necessary in upstate NY. He asked Gunky to drive down the boat launch and out onto the middle of Nature's ice rink. Gunky complied and was in position when the DEI slammed on his brakes from the passenger side. Startled, Gunky over-steered and did a 360 before sliding to a stop. Normal breathing resumed after a while.

The DEI then asked Gunky what he should have done differently. "Ah, steer the other way?" "Correct, you steer in the direction of the skid. Now get this wagon moving up to 20-25 mph and we'll try it again."

Gunky complied and this time when the DEI unexpectedly hit his brakes, Gunky turned the wheels correctly, short-circuiting any sliding spinning and continuing straight across the lake at speed. After a couple more tries, Gunky mastered this quick-reaction driving skill, then returned the car to the center of the lake as directed.

Looking into the back seat, the DEI said, "Your turn." Her response? "You're joking." After some nervous chatter, she got out of the car on the same side as Gunky. As they passed she slipped, but Gunky caught her before she hit the ice. They met face-to-face and their lips brushed briefly. Not a word was spoken as they stared deeply into each other's eyes. She then quietly took her seat behind the wheel. In the rearview mirror Gunky could see a glow in her deep blue eyes.

"Same deal; get up to speed; I'll surprise you with the brakes; and you try to recover." After 15 minutes of spinning and swerving, the men on-board almost needed a barf bag. "One more time" after "One more time" ended in another wild ride. So focused were all on her getting the spin straightened that none noticed how dangerously close the car was getting to the shore. Only after nearly tee-boning a semi-submerged dock-post did the DEI shout, "Time out! We'll get this mastered; that's why we go out here. But I'll take over the wheel from here."

She was red-face embarrassed and quietly climbed to the backseat sitting close to her door. Gunky sat silent and sympathetically near his door on the opposite side. Only a sad glance was exchanged with their eyes.

That Saturday night was the last high-school sock hop at the Town Hall to which everyone just went, no date required. Gunky got there late and was goofing off with his jock friends when he spotted her from across the dance floor. Her beautiful blue eyes were beaming straight at him, for how long he was not aware. Not smart enough to realize her come hither, she strolled a little closer and twinkled at him again. This time, Gunky figured she was saying something, ah, to dance with him? When he looked around, much to his surprise her main squeeze was not to be seen. His buddies egged him on by whispering, "See an opening; why not go for it?"

This was new territory for Gunky, but he waited for the next slow song to ask her to dance. Simply dreamy when she put her arms around his neck. She explained she wanted to thank him for not telling the whole school how badly she drove.

"Most guys would have blabbed about the dumb blond almost wrecking the car on the lake. You're so kind; you didn't. You're special.

When the song ended (too soon!) she said, "Walk with me outside; I need some fresh air." She strolled with him out onto the patio, looked around, and then pulled him into the shadows. After saying, "Thank you" again, she looked into Gunky's eyes, closed hers, and gave him a long slow soft kiss. Magical!

Then the cough. No, not from her, but from the adult male chaperon outside having a smoke. "Kids, the dance is inside, please." She giggled and said to him, "We're done."

Oops! Neither had paid attention to the time because the last song was now playing and her father had already arrived to take her home. "Daddy, this is Gunky; he's in my Driver's Ed class. He's great on ice." Gunky blushed nervously when he heard, "Nice to see you, son."

Because this DE class was the only time they shared alone together in school, the following Thursday could not arrive fast enough for Gunky. He assumed their last lesson would be more practice on the frozen pond. The DEI, however, had something different in mind, driving in traffic. Gunky was up first and comfortably negotiated on-coming cars on the narrow 2-way street made more so by the snow drifts plowed high on either side. When they switched seats for her to drive the car back to the high school, she gave him a secret smile and wink.

Near-hits, not near-misses, again! The farther she drove down the main drag the closer she seemed to get near cars parked on the right. When the Instructor shouted her name, she over-corrected and nearly side-swiped an on-coming car on her left. "Slow down a bit and leave more room on both sides!" Suddenly, another passing car whizzed by way too close for comfort.

In the only time Gunky ever saw him rattled, the DEI shouted, "Stop! What's the matter with you? Are you blind?"

Next was one of those most dramatic, precious, and unforgettable moments. Gunky and the DEI almost needed defibrillators when she replied, "Well, yes, half blind. Because of a childhood accident, my right eye is made of glass."

After that day, she and Gunky remained dear friends, nothing more. She respected Gunky for keeping her secrets and told him often how much she appreciated his gentlemanly discretion.

Upon graduation, both promised to keep in touch as they went off to different colleges, but never did. Time flew and their 20th-class reunion arrived. Everyone in the class of 18 attended but one. Only Gunky knew why.

Out-of-the-blue a month earlier, he had gotten an email from her with an update and a request. Her life story was ever so poignant.

She conveyed she always had an addiction to older men and had married 3, all of whom suddenly died soon thereafter. Her inheritances had afforded her great wealth, no less than three multi-star restaurants, but very little happiness was bequeathed.

She admitted never being really close to anyone in their high-school class, except perhaps Gunky, and deeply regretted staying so detached, especially now. Her heartfelt request, "I'm all alone; say something wickedly funny to me like you used to."

Gunky immediately telephoned the number in Florida on the bottom of her email. When she answered, all he said was, "I suppose you'll claim they all died on you in bed?"

She giggled and said softly that that was a good, but that she knew he could do better. "Make my chest hurt by laughing more than it does now from this terminal curse." Gunky summoned all his wits and then lovingly whispered, "You know, I always liked your right eye better."

Her melancholic reply was, "Perfect; I knew you could do it; if only you had been older than me."

She then said she would forever cherish their one kiss and that forever was about a month.

The reunion of the 17 remaining classmates in that memorable Town Hall had the inevitable moment when someone asked if anyone knew where she was. Gunky then proposed a toast, "Please raise your glass and give a wink to Beautiful Blue Eyes, best driver on ice. BCNU."

If you are wondering, you see you "Never know, do you?

Light the Sky Abla3e! (Behold Upwards)

Skyward approached with anticipation
To view overhead portals to infinity.
Gratification instant, breathtaking.
Perceive the silent dark canopy of delight.
Dearest perforated ink
Shining in or shining out?
Multiplying and revolving.
Dimmest as wondrous as Brights.
Your gifts are transmitted.
Joy and peace to all souls.

    Growing up (still questionable), Gunky anticipated two special events with great expectations. The second was the Turn-of-the-Century, which Gunky, but few in the rest of the World, knew would occur between 2000 and 2001, and would not be partying like it was 1999. The first was the reappearance of the Comet Halley, the object of this adventure.

    Gunky had a young Son with whom he enjoyed exploring nature. One of their hours out amongst the birds and flowers (thanks, Mom) produced an extraordinary collection of leaves from the many different trees in their neighborhood. Without prompting, 7-year old Son taped them onto white sheets of paper; looked up their species in Gunky's Tree Book; then printed their names below each in green ink. Gunky preserved this singular treasure as a keepsake. A quarter century later, Gunky spent hours meticulously removing decomposed tape from each delicate, dried-out leaf; reaffixing them to aged scripted-scrapes of paper; and mounting all into a collage frame. Gunky gave this masterpiece to Son as a 32nd birthday gift, along with a recount of the tale you are about to read, which is tantamount to a long overdue apology.

As the fateful night approached for Halley to reappear in the winter sky of 1986, Gunky shared his joy about finally being able to see his boyhood astronomical dream. Son also got jazzed, so much so he put their boots, coats, and gloves near the back door to the deck so they could dress at a moment's notice on their way outside into the cold still night. They kept their TV turned on at dinner those cold early February nights (a violation of Gunky Family Rules) only to be able to hear when the mighty comet would best be visible.

Then the dramatic announcement, "If you go outside at 6:20 pm tonight and look toward the Western horizon, you will have the best chance of viewing Halley.

Whoa, it's 6:01! In a flurry, they suited up and dashed into the crisp outdoors. Jogging deep into their backyard, they realized too many beautiful trees sky-scraped the horizon. Seeing Son's sad face, Gunky took him by the hand and slowly walked him through their neighbor's back yards to get an open view of the crystal-clear star-filled sky. Four neighbor's west, an unobstructed view awaited them. It was the anticipation of a lifetime.

Son asked Gunky what time it was every minute. After an eternity, Gunky said, "6:20". What they saw next in sheer silence was nothing short of spectacular. It took Gunky's breath away. He squeezed Son's hand in excitement and was startled. Looking down to see an astonished young lad's face, he realized he was holding only a glove with no hand inside!

Peering through the dimly lit backyards, all Gunky could perceive was the outline of the flapping arms and legs of a 4-foot snowsuit bouncing home. Gunky called his name, but the words dropped out of the frigid air and hit the ground two feet from him. Gunky looked back toward the open sky where they had just seen the flash; it was gone. "No surprise", said Gunky smiling to himself as he turned to jog home. Well that was bogus.

On arrival, Gunky found Son shouting with pride, "What a great Pop I have!", and Mom staring at Gunky with arms' crossed and a puzzled look. It was an odd scene. Gunky was enjoying Son's thrill while Mom was suggesting it was time to calm down and get ready for bed because it was a school night. Without further ado, Son hopped upstairs; popped into his jammies; and pooped-out in his bed with a grand smile on his face.

"OK, what did you do to our boy this time?" were the first words out of Mom's grinning mouth. Gunky's tepid reply was that their timing was perfect. "Hmm, to see what? The weatherman said the Halley's Comet Show was a washout. Even at peak brightness, it would appear so faintly you'd probably fail to see its fuzzy glow unless you were outside for an hour to let your eyes to acclimate to the darkness. So please tell me now, what's up?"

Gunky told Mom how they walked through backyards to get an open view of the sky; no problem.

"As soon as we arrived there, a bright light slowly and silently rose above the tree line; arched above the horizon; and then ducked out-of-sight. It was brilliant! When I looked down to see if the Boy had seen it, he was already racing home. Thought it had scared him, but he seems to really have enjoyed it." Knowing Gunky well, Mom remained skeptical, "Try again."

"OK, Dear. Here's what I think happened to the best of my powers of deduction. You know that Air National Guard base up the road? Well, apparently what we saw was the nose light of a chopper taking off. It lifted, hovered, and then turned with its nose dipping down and out of sight. We never heard any sound probably because of the distance and the stiff frigid wind at our backs. Best I can offer."

A little to Gunky's surprise she replied, "Makes sense. Well, the Boy's one happy camper!"

The end? Not so fast! Both Mom and Gunky continued their evening activities, school-homework and work-work, respectively, burning the midnight oil. Their only other interaction with the Boy was to check if he were asleep, which he was with the same big grin on his face.

Next morning, all overslept a bit so it was a mad dash to get the Boy onto the bus; Mom to school; and Gunky to work. The previous night's adventure wasn't mentioned; big mistake.

Later that morning, Mom got a call from Son's teacher. She had asked his class if anyone had seen the comet the night before. "Your son waved his hand shouting, 'I did; I did!'" He then told us he saw a bright flash of light streak across the sky. When the rest of the class dejectedly reported seeing nothing and asked how come he did, your son proudly said, "Well,

MY Dad is a scientist and he knew right where to look." His teacher then said, "It was a fun moment for the whole class. Could you would tell me where exactly your husband took your son to look?"

That night at dinner the Boy recounted giving his class report. Mom and Gunky didn't have the heart to tell him the truth. Turns out, they never did tell him! Hence, the apology accompanying the collage of trees leaves autographed in the young lad's own hand. Priceless!

If you are wondering if what you just thought you saw was a shooting star, recall the wonders of your youth, then go to sleep with a big grin on your face.

MK. Zany (Another Bump in the Night)

You're reading a bizarre and sad affair.
Lions, tigers, and monks were there.
A hungry cat ate a late night snack
And a new critter snuck out from the black.

Beyond a dadow of a shout, "It" is the funkiest Newcomer on Planet Earth for decades. Nessie, Squatch, and Mothy have nothing over Zany. Turns out, perhaps they never will.

A distraught soul became It's unwitting father. Never-before-seen, this critter has been classed as a cryptid, or hypothetical species known from anecdotal evidence insufficient to prove its existence with certainty. Why? Because "They" don't want you to believe It roams freely. Turns out, there's no reason to hide this, except "be-wilder-ment"!

One fall day, the keeper of an exotic wild-animal farm opened all his cages, then died of a heart attack. More than 50 of its denizens ran amuck into the surrounding countryside, mostly lions and lionesses; tigers and leopards; and bears black and grizzly (fess up; you just whispered $L\_\,\_\,\_$ s, $T\_\,\_\,\_\,\_s$ and $B\_\,\_\,\_s$). Authorities alluded to an unknown number of monkeys. Turns out, they may have missed one?

Texts advised those at schools or businesses to shutter and those in cars and homes to shelter until the crisis was resolved. Early on, a leopard, no tigers, and a grizzly (*humming it again?*) plus one monkey were reportedly recaptured unharmed and taken to a nearby zoo. Other seen were shot-on-sight, ineffectively with tranquilizer guns, then massacred by vigilantes firing assault rifles from pickup-truck beds. The interim death toll was 9 lions and 8 lionesses; 18 tigers; 6 black and 2 grizzly bears (*last chance ...Oh my!*); a wolf; and a baboon. In the downpour and dark of the night, unruliness reigned, causing the animal count to become ambiguous. Turns out no one suspected the total might have been unknowingly reduced by one, giving birth to an abominable simian feline of this "tail".

Fast forward a few days when "First Sounds" were heard, which, after initial panic, were dismissed as post-hypnotic suggestion. Local folk who thought they heard something freely conceded, "Nawh, it's just the leaves blowing, trees yawning, and porch floorboards creaking." Turns out no one anticipated these sounds just announced an "Arrival"

Fast forward a few weeks more when "First Signs" appeared, again given only modest notice. They were hood patches appearing on pickup trucks early morning when the locals ventured out to start them up for work. Each looked as if some thing warm had laid on the hood overnight, preventing a thin layer of frost from forming underneath. Sadly, the number brain cells devoted to identifying their origin were few and weak, causing a feature missing from the mysterious marks to go unnoticed. Turns out neither leading to nor from hood patches were prints.

In fairness, these patches did not raise any alarm, because, after all, all sorts of normal animals were known to seek the warmth of engine hoods in winter. Cats first came to mind, domestic and feral. Dogs didn't because most had their own outhouses. Raccoons certainly did not. Last, most other four-legged critters should or would have been in hibernation. Turns out no one thought there might be a new tetrapod in town.

Fast forward further into that brutally cold winter when "Second Signs" appeared. These nocturnal prints were door-handle smudges, appearing on cars and pickups, again conspicuous because of missing frost. They were given a touch more attention than the hood patches because of their possible intent, entry? Local economic times were hard so speculation immediately fixated on the homeless trying to gain shelter, or the criminal trying to boost a vehicle. Sadly, again, mental efforts to decipher the culprit's nature were hampered by not noticing a similar missing link at the scene of the attempted crime. Turns out neither leading to nor from the door-handle smudges were any prints.

Fast forward finally into late December when "Third Signs" materialized, eerie enigmas which finally sounded the alarm. Turns out that while the first two Signs had plausible explanations, the third one had only quirkiness.

With Christmas past, cardboard boxes and dried-out, tinsel-laden evergreens were being deposited near the curbs in front of homes. For thriftiness and tradition, neighbors had arranged for this Holiday refuse to be collected altogether to fuel a mega-bonfire to celebrate New Year's Eve (Can you imagine Gunky's eyes aglow?). Turns out these discards would be too tempting for what maybe was a "New Cat in Town"?

It was Gunky's elderly friend, George, who first recognized the occurrence of these weird phenomena. Turns out, he would become the true "Hero" of this Gunky adventure "tail".

George was a great neighbor, very respectful of everyone's privacy and rights. No one had issues with his self-appointment as local watchman. If you were away, he was the eyes and ears of your home security system. If anything went out-of-place, he noticed, investigated, and reported. He did not miss much, especially the little things. Rumor had it he had the largest collection of solved "Spot-the-Differences" puzzles on Planet Earth, and perhaps others. Turns out he was a most-valuable resource to the local folk as this tail unfolded.

George's aptitude was acute awareness. How else could he have ever noticed that a number of colorful empty gift boxes had disappeared, but had not gone missing? Instead, he astutely observed some had merely been placed inside another. Yes, you heard correctly. Turns out someone or some thing had nested boxes along the curb, stealthily minimizing their number.

"Well, I'll be damned", he mumbled to himself after solving the mystery of the missing boxes. "Who around here is such a neat freak?" Yes, Gunky was on his short list, but George didn't suspect him for a moment. He thought it could be Elsie, his girlfriend. Widower and widow, they enjoyed living together. But George could not ask her. No, not about marriage, about the boxes! Readers, where are minds? Turns out we're talking about nesting, not necking!

All was calm until George sensed something else was different. "Boxes, boxes, where are the boxes, Part 2?" Again, the curbs didn't look quite right to him. First, boxes seemed to be switching from one curb to another. Next, he realized a most-astonishing fact. Not only were boxes being repositioned, they were also being arranged according to color, greens-with-greens; reds-with-reds; etc. Turns out by thinking inside the box (pun intended), he deduced boxes were being color-coordinated in a sort of spectral arrangement.

Yes, you heard correctly again. Turns out no one appreciated the irony of his asking, "What on Earth is doing this?"

Despite his primo powers of observation and deduction, George, too, failed to notice there were any prints going to or coming from anomalies. After all, they had been missing from the hood patches and door-handle smudges. So stupefied by his own discoveries, he had to confide in his trusted friend Gunky. Turns out he had to summon much courage to admit he was baffled given their (and his) strangeness.

While these anomalies were unfolding, "They" finally submitted an official after-action report. Experts had monkeyed around with the number of animals caged, released, recaptured, or killed. Their conclusion was confident, "The public is now safe and can relax because all escaped wild animals have been accounted for." Ironically, their mission statement for the cleanup had been, "No animal will be left behind." However, local, national, and international reporters covering this bizarre event had done their own counting. Their census of the official count differed by 1. Turns out the number was the same as a freaky new conspiracy was born!

George and Gunky then conjured up something very deviant. Their attention zeroed in on the number of cats and monkeys, which had jumped all-around during this circus. Their theory was that one of the big cats got hungry after its escape and munched on a fellow renegade, a monkey. Shortly after its meal of prime-mate (apologies), the satisfied and sleeping cat was spotted; shot with an experimental tranquilizer; and chauffeured to a local vet in critical condition. All available animal blood was called-in for the vital transfusion needed to save its 9th life. Turns out revitalization appeared hopeless, but was it?

Given its expense, no autopsy was performed, and the carcass added to that night's medical waste. No one knew whether these remains ever got to the incinerator. Turns out the trashman, a buddy of George's, told him, "Body bag seemed a tad light, even for a little kitty."

Shortly thereafter, curious George passed away peacefully of natural causes after a grand life. Just before he departed, he privately shared with Gunky his last feelings about these strange occurrences. Seems his 6th sense warned him of a new presence in the neighborhood. Because it was so strong, he had conducted some late-night walkabouts, and heard a strange new sound and saw some sinister shadows. Investigating the scene from where he thought they came, he stepped into the first piece of solid evidence. Turns out it was "Scat, the sight and stink the likes of which he had never seen nor smelled before."

Now to the present. Gunky kept his promise to George to follow-up on his premonition and patty. After nights of surveillance, he tracked an odd print, a hybrid between a hand and paw. Gunky conjectured some combo of chemical in the calmative; genetic ganging of their gores; and pinches of pâté sparked the birth of a new species, which incubated in a zombie-like big-cat's belly. This product would have the charm of a chimp and curiosity of a cat. Turns out, Gunky would christen it a "MonkeyKat" for its bio-blend, and for its enchanting escapades, Zany.

Thus, MK Zany became the latest Freak of Nature. Given its antics, its only apparent reason for living seems to be to amaze and amuse, not alarm. Turns out, MKZ is a benevolent beast, not a malevolent monster.

If you are wondering if Gunky is aiding-and-abetting a mild and crazy thing that trots about urban canyons, look for "It's" likeness on pet-food boxes, cereal bowls, tee shirts, and coffee mugs as advertised on syndicated (sorry) late-night cable TV. And if you call now, "Your species will be doubled and we'll even include a sample of simulated scat; meow."

Naughty Boots
(Dressed to Scrum)

Let me display my first love!
Let my life force entertain!
Let my music sing now!
It is my time!
Be in my moment!
Let passion ignite!
This defines me!
Civility explodes!
Feel the joy!
Thrills rise!
Love emerges!
Placed on high!
All sport!
All music!
Beautiful!

Gunky has often been accused, at times many times, of re-repeating himself. He's doubly sure he doesn't, but if he did, and he doesn't, listeners would have to endure a repeat no more than thrice or more. Sometimes repeating causes precious, precious, precious moments.

Gunky has a Daughter, whom, from time-to-time, has had different nicknames. She was a special child and now a beautiful adult, especially in spirit and soul. If there was one gene Gunky passed on to her it was the one coded *adventure-seeker.* She was not afraid to boldly go where no Gunky has not yet or ever gone before.

One day she came home from grade school and announced to Mom and Gunky she wanted to play a musical instrument. Not being able to decide which, she learned to play both the flute and violin extraordinarily very well!

One night Gunky was down in the family room listening to an early violin practice session. After playing for about a half-hour, she asked her Dad how she was doing. Gunky, of course, said it was beginning to sound like music. "Any advice?" All Gunky said was, "Sounded a tad squeaky, Squeaky." She smiled and agreed, somewhat.

At bedtime, all Gunky whispered was, "Goodnight, Squeaky", and kissed her forehead. Somehow, don't understand why, this nickname stuck.

Practices continued and her improvement was clear. One night, after a particularly well-played medley, she was walking upstairs to do her homework when she stopped and asked the same question. All Gunky said was, "Child of the Night. What music you make."

For those who don't know, this is a variation of a quote from the most evil vampire ever portrayed as he was walked up stone stairs to the wails of wolves outside (thank you, Bela). Needless-to-say, it has been claimed, falsely so, that this compliment was repeated repeatedly whenever she played especially well, which was frequent and often.

One night Gunky mentioned to Mom that his company was hosting a musical talent contest for its staff. He wondered out loud if that would be something Daughter might be interested in doing. Before Mom could respond with, "No, she's too young", oops! Seems the little child of theirs was sitting around the corner in the living room. "I'd like to try."

The day of the contest into to the vast auditorium she, her violin, and Gunky went. The hall was beautiful, as was the competition. Just before she was to take the stage, she leaned over and asked Gunky for some last-minute advice. "Play music, my dear, not just the notes." Onto the stage bounced the youngest and most chronologically challenged competitor.

First up was a song from the list of 10 distributed to all before the competition. They selected #6. Without hesitation, she stepped up and played. Only one short passage was a bit squeaky, but all in the room heard her do some beautiful improvising. WOW!

Second up was to be a surprise the judges would select for her to sight-read and play. When they announced the title by putting the sheet music on her stand, she smiled politely. Again, she surprisingly stepped up and played the song almost from memory; it had been one of her favorites to practice. Nailed it. WOW, WOW!

Last up was the finale, a song she would select. All she did was close her eyes and make it her own. She slowed down the tempo from the traditional pace and played beautiful music. Not a dry eye in the audience, especially those on her proud Dad. WOW, WOW, WOW!

Arriving home, Mom Gunky asked how she did. Her reply "Had fun, made 100 bucks!"

When it came to the flute, she practiced only if and when she wanted. She took it with her to college where she majored in Spanish. She did put her talents to good use when self-exiled to South America for 6 months of total immersion.

Not long after the American delegation landed, she learned they had enough instruments in their contingent for a mini-ensemble, and began to play together for fun. Overhearing them, their chaperon asked, "Do you play events?" They then traveled playing weddings and parties, with their pay leftovers from uneaten elegant dinners.

This experience was well worth it; there was no better way to learn a language. It paid off when she moved to way out West. Her occupation there was the same as at home, bank teller. When a promotion opportunity opened, she called her Dad to ask how to respond to some of questions an interviewer would ask. She said the entire interview would be in Spanish and the position was heavily competed. After cogitating a bit, Gunky suggested something she might try. Sure enough, when she was asked in Spanish, "Why should I hire you?" Her reply was, "I also speak English very well" in English! Needless-to-say, she was hired on the spot! Brillante; aravilloso!

Now back to this adventure and its opening haka. Daughter was a well-grounded individual, but also had some Gunky traits. One night she called from college to say, "Hey Dad, guess what? I'm a hooker now." This was the lead-in to a word game she and Gunky played often. Give a cryptic clue and the listener had to guess the context. Gunky laughed out loud. He had no worries about Daughter going astray, but was slightly stymied and hesitated. "Want a hint? I learned what dirt tasted like today." (hooted earlier by Gunky in "Close Encounters"). Hearing him answer, "Rugby", all she could say was, "That's my Dad."

She then told Dad the venue for her last match that season was at home. The other good news was the game was mid-afternoon, just before her last concert that night. She asked if Mom and Gunky could come see and hear her play in both. Road trip double-header!

She was tenacious in mauls, rucks, and scrums. After a knock-down, drag-out, but fair match, nary any of her not covered in muck. Ladies on both teams had some real down-and-dirty fun.

Mom and Gunky were charmed arriving in the magnificently ornate chapel auditorium and stunned after reading the program. She never told them she was to be a soloist for this prestigious wind ensemble! When her time came at the end of the program, she stepped out front stage center in a beautiful full-length black gown and played her magical flute. Her virtuoso performance received a standing ovation not started by her Mom or Dad. Applause, encore applause, and proud tears of joy!

As a college senior, this would be her last performance. After her fellow musicians had said their tearful goodbyes and were collecting their instruments, Gunky couldn't help but notice her dawdling in the center of the stage, intermittently glancing back at him. When their eyes finally connected, she carefully looked around; put her index finger to her lips; and glanced down. With only Mom and Gunky watching (really), she lifted her gown high enough to reveal she was still wearing her muddy rugby boots! Seems she had forgotten to bring her formal dress shoes. How her; how Squeaky!

If you are wondering what Gunky hums to himself when he hears a squeak or gets mud on his boots it's "Sweet child of mine" (credit Guns N' Roses).

Only Gunk (Ode of O)

Ology of om, out, or op.
Obligatory one on one.
Observe only outcome.
Omnishamble or Opus?

Oscitating on the orderliness of these oratories, Gunky overtly offers one occasion to overcome an oppilation. Opposed to ongoing the obtuse opening, Gunky objected other options for an oratory originating with the 15th letter. One other was an ohmage to orange to the optical output of his occupation (fireballs) or the obvious orb on the orisont (as in "Ever Rising"). Oscillating over 7000 options, Gunky outwent oneself to orchestrate an orgy of O's to ordain it as an ordinal. Optimistic at the onset, Gunky's obviously been outwitted by ornery opposition.

Overdone?

To restart, Gunky offers the following alternate O-minus tale, okeydokey?

Gunky fondly recollects many events during the decade of ups-and-downs caring for wife Petruskha. Because of her worsening physical condition, she had to put her active lifestyle on hold (no more scuba, sky, or soccer diving). Her replacement became needlepoint, an activity requiring one to sit still a long time, not in her DNA. One night they were downstairs in the family room relaxing after dinner, eaten mostly by Gunky. After discussing the state of the World, she returned to her project and Gunky to his re-reading of the complete writings of Sherlock Holmes.

Gunky couldn't help notice her fidget. She would look between the needlepoint and its instructions; mutter something under her breath; sigh; and then continue to stich. It was only after she repeated this series of actions several times that she stopped and stared at Gunky with "Xs" in her eyes. She then asked what seemed a bizarre, but possibly logical, question.

"You need a calculator and a ruler?" Gunky answered in response.

"This pattern is all out-of-whack. Colors of the threads don't match; lines seem crooked; and number of stiches doesn't add up. Somebody really botched this design. Frustrating. I'll try to work it out. I'll just have to apply the few brain cells I've left. Won't be perfect."

Her body language then suggested the needlepoint was not to be viewed. Gunky guessed it probably was being prepared as a homemade present for his upcoming birthday.

This mini-drama was repeated the next evening and the next. It ended when she looked at Gunky and said, "May I ask you a question?" Gunky's reply did not stray from his usual drenched-in-sarcasm demeanor, "Yes, and you may ask a second one."

The smirk Gunky got in return was beautiful. "What's the name of that running joke you scientists have about your experiments not working when they should; it's some sort of law? Seems to in effect with my project, which, because of all its glitches, will never get done by tomorrow. Might as well show it to you now."

With her permission, he got up and strolled over to see "Y" she was so troubled. Upon viewing the product of her thoughtful labors, he put his hand on her shoulder and said, "Looks fine just the way it is now. It's simply brilliant. Gunk will take it."

If you are wondering, GunkY still has that perfect prepared needlepoint, not because of the joke Murph played on his nearly-impossible-to-trick late wife, but because every letter, there or not, was stitched with her own hands and with all her love. Priceless!

Please & Thank You, Ma'am, a Gentleman Makes? (Down the Creek)

Born to be mild or born to be wild?
It's always an accident of birth.
Live to smile or live to rile?
All will depend on mirth.

Who should you, can you, and/or do you respect and trust?

"It would be a great mistake to ever respect and/or trust anyone solely because someone merely told you to do so." Here is why this is one of Gunky "Rules for Living".

As Gunky has said many times, he considers himself fortunate to have had grown up (?) during perhaps the most tumultuous time in modern history, the '60s. Great issues needed resolution: Black v. White, Woman v. Man, Pollution v. Breathing, and War v. Peace. Although over-simplified, don't all of these conflicts reduce to respect? Enough sermonizing. You've already read a tale involving the watershed moment called Woodstock, a happening in which Gunky, his wife-to-be, and parents participated in by default. Realize that adventure had a subliminal subplot, Authority v. Rights. This story, from same massive weekend, is about Bikers v. Elders.

Gunky grew up a skin head. Not what you're thinking again! Grandpa was a barber. To make life simple, he always cut Gunky's hair "good enough" to never need a comb. Price was right. Gunky really liked going to "The Shop" because Grandpa sold parakeets from the back room. What marvelous colors and amazing cacophony of sounds! Whenever Gunky is in a pet store, the smell of birds reminds him of those quaint old times and he smiles.

If you recall the number of kids in Gunky's high school class, you'll appreciate just how small his town really was; only a 4-way blinking traffic light was needed. Gunky often joked with his college buddies about what would happen if he secretly left of his dorm room any time day or night; drove 4 hours toward his childhood home in someone's borrowed car; abandoned it a half-mile away; camouflaged himself; crawled through the back woods into his Pop's garage; hid under a tarp; and then picked his nose. Over coffee the next morning at the only diner in town, locals would debate how much, how slimy, how sticky, and what color the residue was stuck on which finger. But we digress. Need to switch from boogers back to bikers and bums.

From an early age, you may have been given similar guidance. "They are the pillars of our community, our town elders, who command your unquestioning respect. Whenever they pass you are to bow your head slightly and address them as Madam or Sir. You can only hope to be as fortunate to grow up and be like them."

It was the Saturday afternoon of Woodstock and the heat and humidity made it pure Hell. Gunky, Older Brother, Mom, and Pop were sitting on lawn chairs on their front porch watching the World pass by. They saw just about everything you could imagine clothes-wise, from white tee-shirts and tan shorts-to-psychedelic robes-to-all skin. The endless parade of concert goers struggling to hike between roadblocks from the bottom of the hill to the Promised Land of Free Love was nothing short of spellbinding. All sorts of people were accompanied by the happy noises of blissful camaraderie.

This free entertainment was in full sight and sound when Gunky's clan first heard rolling thunder. It started out low, then crescendoed to ear-splitting levels. It came not from up in the sky above, but down from the hill below.

The source soon revealed itself, a pack of motorcycles slowly and carefully negotiating its way through the exodus. Upon seeing their leader's arm raise, silence returned, and all the bikes came to a halt on the opposite side of the low hedge that separated the road from Gunky's front yard. The dozen or so riders dismounted, looked around, and then started strolling toward the porch. At that moment, the atmosphere switched from carefree to up-tight.

Gunky, his Mom, Pop, and Older Brother immediately stopped talking and looked at each other. Pop spoke first, calmly directing an order to Gunky, "Get the rifle."

Gunky first thought Pop was kidding and gave a wise-ass reply, "But Pop, we only have one shell." Without hesitation, Pop calmly issued a second command, "Get it, too."

When Gunky looked back toward the hedge he realized it was too late to take any action and froze in his chair. The lead biker had arrived and was looking at all them over the shoulder-high railing. This hulk of a beast was soon followed by his gang, the scuzziest, orneriest, and most ruthless-looking pack of thugs who ever knuckle-dragged upright on the Planet.

Afterwards, all would admit they thought they were going to be raped and murdered, with the pain high and death slow. But who else but Mom to the rescue!

Putting his naked-lady and skull-and-crossbones-tattooed stitches-ridden filthy arm on the railing, the leader, in a quiet, pleasant voice asked, "Ma'am, we'd be riding a long way and we's a-mighty thirsty. Could we trouble you good folks for a drink of water? We'd pay. Town's dry."

Mom's miracle working began with a sweet reply, "Love to boys; won't be a minute!" Now Gunky has shared earlier about how time either flies or stalls in certain situations. In this episode, time went both ways. For Pop, Older Brother, and Gunky, it was a lifetime, pun intended. For Mom, it was a blink, less than 2 minutes elapsed time.

Into the kitchen empty-handed and back onto the porch in a flash carrying nothing less than a large, chilled-crystal pitcher of lemonade on a silver tray and a dozen of her best goblets. She put her serving down on a table on the porch and began pouring. After she filled each glass, she handed it over the railing to each critter, ah biker, who had politely lined up to receive their cold beverage. Almost nothing was said as each drained their glasses; wiped their mouths with their forearms; and gave thanks with a belch.

"Thank ya kindly, Ma'am. Whadda we owe ya?" Mom's reply was delightful, "Why, not a penny; it's our pleasure." Without hesitation, the leader said, "Well then, we need be moving on."

With that, the gang returned to their bikes, kick-starting each with a roar and cloud of smoke. Their leader was the last to walk away. He was almost to his impressive machine when he stopped, seeming to remember something, turned slowly around, then strolled almost back to the porch, where breathing had ceased again.

Eyeballing the Gunky Clan, he raised a bulging arm and pointed a cautionary finger. "Watch out, good folk. There's some ruthless people running around this here concert. You be safe." With that, he returned to his hog, cranked the engine, and with his wave, all rode off up the road.

To this day, Gunky always wondered if, after giving his stern warning and turning away, that the good biker didn't have the biggest of grins on his face. Doesn't matter. Seems he was right

After that fantastic or disastrous weekend, whichever your point-of-view, it was learned that the pillars of the community had indistinguished themselves by selling, for a buck-a-cup, warm water to several very thirsty concert-goers passing by on foot. This would have been bad enough by itself, but then it was learned this water was not from their faucets, but from the brook ruling behind the elders' houses. The flow may well have been spring-fed, but everyone in the neighborhood had an aging septic tank.

In the end, it was Mom who summarized the experience best, "What a nice young man. He called me Ma'am. Hope they'll be safe, too."

If you are wondering who Gunky respects, this tale provides a life-lesson; hope you learned it also. Peace.

Quintessentially Wonderful Times (Believe!)

They were kwazy and so kooky,
And extraordinarily wooky,
And sometimes very spooky,
Gunky's misadventures!

Gunky never had nor never will have a mid-life crisis; he would be damned. Instead, he decided to stop asking the most-dangerous of rhetorical questions, **"So, what worse could happen next?"**

He learned his lesson in 1999 after **"The International Year of the Gunky"**.

He and his young wife were poor, ambitious graduate students, studying hard to complete their degrees; go out into the real world; and do good work. The campus was a sanctuary from their spartan apartment. Their most-valued possessions were books, books, and more books! They cherished learning and engaging in technical, philosophical, and silly conversations with intellectuals and pseudos. They ran together each day to stay fit. Gunky would spot his partner a lap then try to catch to her before she ran four. They occasionally cooled down by sharing a scoop of ice cream. They would finish it then throw the cup away before returning to their dump of an apartment so as to not leave any sweets for the resilient hungry cockroaches.

Mid-January, Gunky was awakened late one night by what he thought was the alarm for the elevator opposite their 2nd floor apartment door. The smell of smoke immediately convinced him otherwise. After feeling the inside of the door was cool, he raced back into the bedroom to shake and wake up his wife, who was having issues hearing and in a deep sleep. On the way in, he grab their winter coats, hats and boots. When donned, he took her by the hand to the door, under which smoke was now leaking.

Decision time! He cracked open the door slightly and saw an exit through the haze but no flames. After taking deep breaths, they bolted to the top of the stairs, with Gunky pounding on doors shouting, "Fire!" Down they flew outside into fresh air. Not knowing what to do, they copied what others were, sitting in their cars in the parking lot to stay safe and warm.

After giving thanks for their escape, they followed the progress of the fire by watching their balcony. Billowing smoke was first light and white; then fuzzy and gray; and then heavy and black. Soon, it was mushrooming out of all the balconies, 2nd floor and above.

The local fire department arrived within minutes and set up their equipment expertly amongst the piles of snow and rows of cars. They had obviously rehearsed, which paid off. The most dramatic scene was when an ancient woman came out onto her 7th floor balcony wearing only a nightgown and screamed, "My mother; save my mother!" With precision, brave firemen quickly positioned and climbed their aerial ladder, rescuing both within minutes. Impressive!

Couple hours later they were allowed back into their apartment to inspect the damage. It looked like the inside of a coal mine. Everything of value, which was practically nil, was lost. Precious books stunk of smoke and had to be discarded. Sad. Their limited wardrobe of secondhand clothes was washable and recoverable. One item that oddly experienced little damage was the loose-leaf notebook containing the hand-written-in-pencil 1st-draft of Gunky's PhD dissertation, which he still has today. Other occupants in that apartment complex lost much more, making Gunky and wife appreciate their circumstances even more.

This fire was actually the second in a week in that university town. There would be 11 more on subsequent weekends, all arsons, which mysteriously ended in late May. No suspect was ever apprehended. The not-so-funny theory was the arsonist graduated and moved away.

So, what could be worse than fire?

After surviving temporary student housing the next few nights, Gunky and wife relocated into new digs, a basement apartment. This dump was much better than the one they were burned out of because there were fewer bugs. They had friendly student neighbors in the 2 other rentals below deck, as well as respectful merchants topside who operated a flooring store and music shop. Most importantly, this apartment was quiet, unlike their previous one.

Late-January, Gunky was awakened late one night by a groaning sound. He didn't have a clue as to why. At dawn he discovered the noise was from water pipes exposed to the brutal cold in the open stairwell. The good news, none burst and all thawed by that afternoon.

So, what could be worse than freezing?

Mid-March, Gunky was awakened late one night by the sound of dripping water, which he thought might be coming from the leaky bathroom shower. Not! Stepping out of bed, his bare leg was greeted by cold water up to his knee. Yuck! Their bed had been silently transformed into an island by water leaking in at baseboard level. Surprisingly, this inside flood would subside within a few hours. Because they didn't have much else to lose in this disaster, and had no opportunity to relocate, they cleaned up the mess; put their meager belongings up high; and persevered.

So, what could be worse than flooding?

Glorious warm and dry springtime weather eventually returned to upstate NY that May. As occurs annually, campus activities slow as undergraduates finish finals and begin their exodus home for the summer. Because it was typically quiet around their apartment, Gunky failed to notice it had actually gotten even quieter. He did notice a sign announcing the relocation of the flooring and music stores to more profitable locations. He surmised that students in the other apartments had moved out as evidenced by all the trash spilling out of their common dumpster.

Mid-May, Gunky was awakened late one night by the sound of someone pounding on his front door. When he went to check, he was shocked to see the maul of a sledgehammer breach the door. Instinctively, he picked up his 18-inch length of clear, hard, lightweight, plastic tubing, aka, Thumper. As the door splintered open, he waited by the side to hide to "meet and greet" the intruder. Mom was already on the phone calling the police.

In full-survival mode, he pounced on the primary perpetrator penetrating his personal property. He tackled the unwitting body around the neck from behind and face-slammed it into the floor. Grandma never knew what hit her! As Gunky turned, he saw Grandpa standing behind and whacked him across the knees with Mr. Stick, flooring him. Gunky then saw the Grandchildren staring down the stairwell. With eyes aflame he roared, "Who's next?" and chased them up and out into the parking lot. When he got to the top of the stairs, he saw more family, not in work clothes, but in casual shirts and slacks. "Now what?"

Gunky laughed in the face of the suit who stepped forward and threatened, "I'll have arrested for assault". Gunky defiantly countered with, "Go ahead and try; cops are on the way."

The mouthpiece's smirk waned at the sound of sirens. A State Trooper a block away had intercepted the call in his patrol car and responded. The next siren was the local sheriff and the third the ambulance Gunky's wife had called to get care for the bloody-faced old woman and limping old man, both of whom she may have kicked a couple of times in self-defense.

After the usual commotion as to who was in-charge, had jurisdiction, and should be talking, Gunky testified to what had happened and surrendered his piece. The alleged attorney again pleaded, "My men were attacked without provocation by this madman!" Just as the local officer ordered everyone to calm down and go downtown to take statements, out staggered Grandma and Grandpa with hands-up and Petruskha pointing a broomstick at their backs! She stared the lawyer in the eyes and asked, "How did our front door get smashed in? She then directed her attention to the cops stating, "I'm not using Granny's sledgehammer as my defensive weapon because I didn't want to interfere with her prints on it; it's downstairs." Calmer and more contrite words were then communicated by the culprits.

So what was the story? The property on which the complex was built had been sold a month earlier to make way for a pioneering fast-food shop.

Somehow, every occupant but one (guess who?) had been informed the building was condemned and would be demolished by the end of May. The new owners had assumed all the student occupants were undergraduates and would be leaving by then for the summer. Both businesses upstairs were moving to new locations on the owners' other properties. The invaders were subcontractors given permission by the owner to pillage the plumbing and paneling, ah recycle the copper and finished wood before demolition. They claimed they did not know anyone was still living there. Guess again!

At dawn the same day at the police station, the owner's attorney eventually conceded that his employees were in the wrong. They agreed on the facts based on the splinters and, "No comment", to Gunky's questions as to, "Why was the raid conducted in the dead of night?" The owner offered Gunky and Petruskha one of his two-bedroom apartments rent-free for 6 months if they dropped their charges and moved out within 24 hours using a rental truck he would provide for free. University general counsel representing Gunky advised they accept this offer, which would put a happy ending this unsavory episode.

Gunky picked up a rental truck later that afternoon, which he and his wife loaded in less than 2 hours. They then drove to their new apartment nearby and unloaded their belongings in about the same time. Exhausted from this ordeal, they decided to get some sleep and return the truck next morning. Their new apartment was bigger, brighter, and bugless, and best of all, was on the first floor.

Next morning, they took a detour returning the rental truck to drive pass their old haunts one last time. Whoa! The entire building was gone and all that remained was a huge hole in the ground! Guess they weren't fooling about getting that new fast-food joint built, which by the way, was completed less than a month later. About a month after it opened, Gunky and Petruskha went there to eat just-for-kicks. Thumper accompanied them, but did not order anything.

So, what could be worse than fright and fight?

Mid-June, Gunky was awakened late one night by the young couple upstairs, an argument whose mutual screaming indicated it might get violent. He then saw flashing lights outside and knew someone had already called the police. When he went into kitchen for a drink of water, he saw Petruskha standing in front of the kitchen sink. In full voice he said, "Oh well, maybe their fights will end tonight." Petruskha didn't react. Seeing her in her negligence, ah nightgown, Gunky gave a cat-call, to which she also did not respond. When she turned around on her own, she was spooked to see Gunky standing behind her, saying, "Don't scare me like that!"

Recall in the fire episode Petruskha had hearing issues and had not been awoken by the alarm. In the time since, her hearing loss had exacerbated (Gunky is just showing off his vocabulary). In reality, she was nearly deaf. They both agreed it was time to see a doctor.

The diagnosis had good news and bad news. The good was she was pregnant (no surprise; planned). The bad was she had otosclerosis, or hardening of the tiny bones in the middle ear, a condition causing hearing loss sometimes aggravated by pregnancy. As she then joked, "Now I have one thing in common with Beethoven, Howard Hughes, and Frankie Valli."

The doctor's recommendation was she have a stapedectomy in one ear right away and in the other ear 3-6 months after her baby was born. The operation seemed straightforward, much like removing and replacing parts by a car mechanic, but a tad more delicate.

They were warned of some restrictions and complications. Depriving her scuba and sky diving for 12 months presented no problems. Taste disturbance and ringing were low probability risks worth taking to have most hearing restored at high probability. "Let's do this!"

Brave Petruskha and concerned Gunky arrived at hospital for the 5 am surgery. After prep, she and other patients having the same procedure were lined up on the right, pre-op, side of the corridor, which Gunky could see through a window. At her expected return time, Gunky looked again and saw her in the same spot with her surgeon by her side. Seeing Gunky, he came to the door and explained the delay. "First two patients had very hard ear bones, so we had to blast." While some might not appreciate this dark humor, Gunky and Petruskha thought it reassuring. Doc then added she was up next and that he had run out of sticks of dynamite.

Three hours later, there she was, on the left, recovery-side, of the corridor. When Gunky leaned close to her and whispered, "How'd it go?", her reply said it all, "Don't shout."

She had 95% recovery of hearing in her right ear and suffered none of the complications. The Doc said he would see her again in about 9 months to fix her left ear so the both Gunky and she could hear their first newborn cry in stereo.

So, what could be worse than failed hearing?

Mid-September, Gunky was awakened late one night feeling indescribably uncomfortable. He had had minor back problems all his life, inherited from both parents, and may have exceeded his physical limits moving into their new home. He nudged Petruskha, and when she woke, said, "I can't feel my feet."

To the ER Petruskha drove Gunky where the university football physio displayed a brutally honest bedside manner, which Gunky and Petruskha respected. "I've not seen such nerve involvement in my career; you'll be lucky to walk." To which Gunky replied, "What, do I win a prize?" The Doc's confident response, "Yes, my skills as your surgeon." The Doc then looked at Petruskha and said, "Happy to see you're with child; depending upon the damage done by the ruptured disc in your husband's back, that could be your only one."

Petruskha and Gunky agreed, "Let's have the surgery; we've nothing to lose." Doc nodded. That brilliant neurosurgeon, who removed the ruptured disc, would send a congratulatory note 4 years later on the birth of Daughter with the muddy boots. Gunky refereed soccer for 25 years thereafter, including the Over-40 women's COWS league (Centrally Organized Women's Soccer-*GOT YA!*), in which Petruskha played and almost got cautioned by him.

So, what could be worse than failed feelings in your feet?

Mid-December, Gunky was awakened late one night by Petruskha who said she was ready to give birth to their one and only Son, the comet gazer. As alluded to in her lead letter, the trip to hospital that dark stormy night was smooth except for the bumpy landing upon parking. Labor took the duration of a soccer match (90 minutes), the same as it would take for Daughter. Gunky was in the delivery room the entire time and watched the beauty and drama unfold. Being a scientist, he became concerned when signals and sounds from monitors slowed in frequency each time Petruskha pushed. Didn't seem quite right. Reason was the umbilical cord was wrapped around the baby boy's neck. The attendants were ready and almost going to take action when out popped a blue baby who was handed over to Gunky.

Then, right before his very eyes, his beautiful baby boy coughed; starting breathing deeply; turned from blue to pink; and shat brown slime all over him. Tears and towels! Joyous!

So, what could be worse than having these fabulous fates?

Dare to ask, again?

There's an adage about not having enough time to do something right the first time, but having the time to do it over. So, here we go again!

To repeat the opening, Gunky never had a mid-life crisis; he would be damned. Why? He again asked the most-dangerous rhetorical question, **"What worse could happen next?"**

He regained his lesson in 2001 after **"The 2nd International Year of the Gunky.**

In July, Gunky got a phone call one Thursday from his company's switchboard. Someone with his last name made a cold call and asked if Gunky worked there. The operator wanted to know how to handle this unexpected call. When she mentioned the caller's first name, Gunky went into shock, but recovered enough to have the call forwarded to his office phone. Chilling!

So far, you have not been introduced to Gunky's Younger Brother. Actually, he is a full-brother, whereas Older is only a half-brother (different Mom, as in "Jinx"). Younger Brother had a tumultuous upbringing. He hung out with the wrong crowd in high-school, aka, dropouts, then followed their example by flunking out. He began a recovery by earning a GED. Next, he joined the US Navy. He was doing well as a cook until he accidentally cut off 1½ fingers when his ship hard-docked and was given a medical discharge. Next, bricklayer. He strayed across the country job-to-job; bottle-to-bottle; and someone else's wife-to-someone else's. The good news is that while he drank heavily and fooled around widely, he never did drugs nor produce any illegitimate offspring. Whew; blessings!

Mom and Pop Gunky always wondered and worried what went wrong. After all, they had raised him the same way as their two other sons, who seemed to turn out OK. What happened?

Younger Brother was a wanderer, clever at covering his tracks and almost impossible to locate. He disappeared from Gunky's view August 27, 1972. He did call home twice. The first was in 1996 before the Holidays, when he called, got Pop, and asked how Mom was doing. Pop told him Mom had been dead for two years. Then second was in 2000, again before the Holidays, when he called, got Older Brother, and asked how Pop was doing. Older Brother told him that Pop had been dead for 2 years, and sadly, to never call him again. Younger Brother obeyed.

When the Internet began to have functionality, Gunky would spend time late at night scanning lists of prisoners and death certificates to learn if he had disappeared for those reasons. Older Brother and Gunky considered hiring a private detective to find him, but decided to not.

Gunky did glean some evidence via cold calls from irate husbands and creditors asking the whereabouts of his Younger Brother. He would ask the callers in what city the wife or money had been grabbed to try and trace his movements. Gunky would then categorically deny he knew anything and volunteered to work with the caller to help find him, really.

As executor of the family estate, Gunky was obligated to find the only other remaining survivor to award him his monetary inheritance, albeit a pittance.

When the Internet really became informative, Gunky spent more late nights surfing same last names and their addresses. BINGO? One night he discovered a person with the same first, middle, and last name with a son named after Gunky who was living in Missouri. Gunky was emotionally paralyzed learning this, and asked Petruskha what he should do. "Call him…now!"

Gunky took some time to prepare an opening request. He practiced out loud exactly what he'd say. "Hello, my name is Gunky. This is a cold call to you because we share the same last name. I'm trying to contact my younger brother, from whom I have not heard in years. I am not selling anything. You have every right to hang up right now. I'll understand, but I am desperate for any information on his whereabouts. I need to find him for important family reasons. Please consider helping me. Thanks for listening."

Petruskha was sitting on the stairway watching as Gunky went live. He gave this speech in as calm and sincere manner as he could. It was met with silence….then… incredible!

"Thank y'all, but I knows I's a brotha, but youse ain't MY brother."

Gunky was speechless (rare!); so was Petruskha who heard this over the speaker phone.

This gentleman stranger had immediately understood Gunky's dilemma and pain, and gave his best to graciously defuse the tension. He had no useful information and offered an apology. Gunky told him that was definitely not necessary. They amused each other with tales about the different branches of their family trees. Both wished their respective families good health and happiness. In truth, they were brothers.

Back to the call on-hold, now being connected by the hotline operator. The voice was recognizable despite the decades. Gunky asked how he was doing. All Younger Brother said was that his boss had asked him one day if he had any living relatives. "I worried that you might be dead, too, now. Also sort of remembered that you were smart, a scientist, and what state you lived in. Hearing this, my boss guessed where you probably worked, so I called its number and now I'm talking to you." What a fluke, but a good one! GAME!

Younger Brother asked a lot of questions about his long-lost family, which Gunky answered fully, but coldly. Who avoided whom? His answers to Gunky were evasive, especially about what he'd been doing for decades and where he was speaking from right then. All Gunky got him to reveal was he was a journeyman bricklayer building a chain of well-known convenience stores around the country. He claimed to never to have been in trouble with nor was running from the law and that he had fathered any illegitimate kids. His explanation for his lost time was that he once got hit in the head by a cinderblock while working as a non-union scab and lost his memory. He started drinking because of the pain. He then abruptly said he had to go because his smoking break was over, and hung up.

That night, on a hunch, Gunky went on-line and searched building permits for this store chain. BINGO! There was one in a town 2-hour's drive south! This and that he said he called when he heard Gunky might be in the same state were suggestive, but not much to go on. Petruskha then suggested, "Why not drive there and see what you can find out?"

The following Saturday, Gunky did just that knowing it was a long-shot. He found the site without difficulty. Problem was, no one was there. Walking around, he noticed there was only one company name on all the equipment. He discovered a truck with a bumper sticker on it advertising this company was hiring drivers and listing a phone number. SET!

Gunky called the number right there and then. To his surprise, the foreman of the company answered. Gunky asked if his Younger Brother worked for him. "Who wants to know? You a bill collector or private dick?" Gunky used his best street talking to convince this guy he didn't want to hurt Younger Brother, only to give him his inheritance, no fooling. At perhaps a weak moment, the tough foreman muttered his company may have been staying at a certain motel. He said he would deny this leak if anyone ever asked. Did this because he liked Younger Brother. MATCH!

Gunky drove to the named motel, went to the front desk, and asked the receptionist to call his room. As soon as Gunky identified himself, Younger Brother hung up. Gunky then took a position in the lobby so he could see the exits to both the elevator and stairway. From the thumping sounds, Gunky knew in advance from which door Younger Brother would exit. Get ready!

You may recall from other chronicles that Gunky admitted to sometimes being stunned. Who Gunky would see next would give him one of the worst shocks of all time!

The person emerging from the door in 2001 was POP, or what Pop looked like when Gunky last saw Younger Brother in 1972 as Best Man at his wedding with Petruskha! Chills just ran down Gunky's spine again writing this.

After an awkward reunion in the lobby, Gunky suggested Younger Brother join him for lunch at a fast food joint nearby; he accepted. Younger Brother continued to be cleverly evasive about his past life and whereabouts. When the bill came, Younger Brother offered to pay and opened his wallet wide. Gunky immediately noticed his driver's license was showing and took a snapshot of it in his mind's eye, a talent he used often in his both his vocation and avocation. Upon seeing Gunky staring at his wallet, Younger Brother snapped it shut in anger. Gunky gave him his inheritance check, which sadly, he probably drank later that night.

Knowing Younger Brother was not ready nor willing to come-to-terms with his deserting his family, they parted ways. Before leaving, Gunky got a kind stranger to take a photo of them together. Side-by-side with one of Pop, you'd swear they were the same person.

Gunky made a deal with his then boss to keep an eye on him and to call Gunky if any emergency ever happened that he should know about. The boss agreed, but was never heard from again. From information memorized from seeing his driver's license, Gunky knew where Younger

Brother lived. He tracked his whereabouts after that dramatic, heart-wrenching day.

About 10 years later, Gunky learned from the Veterans Administration that Younger Brother's health was failing quickly. He would pass away at age 63 before Gunky could see him again. A sad chapter in Gunky's life ended sadly. May he rest in Peace.

So, what could be worse than losing your brother?

No more; enough!

If you are wondering why Gunky never had a depression, drinking, drug-abuse, or violent-rage problem because of all the stress from these episodes, why should he have had?

Rx, by Dr. Gunky (Easy)

Keep Calm and Gunky On!

Gunky's cited age is often doubted, not only because of the manner in which he acts but also by the way he appears. Attributes invoking disbelief with regard to the latter are the ownership of a full, thick head of dark hair and fair, wrinkle-free of skin. Gunky always pleads that he looks so young because he has had little stress in his life (Ha!).

After you grow old enough to retire and piss away smidgeons of your spare time surfing the Net, you will be exposed to an inordinate number of inane lists. In their honor, here is one with "Gunky Rules", which may contribute to his looking chronologically challenged? It, too, has been alphabetized, with the 26 annotated to the extent to which Gunky follows them. He provides this list for illumination only, not proselytization; one size does not fit all.

Always speak benevolently, lovingly, respectfully, and truthfully (Work in progress).

Beware of social media, because its use can cause more family/friend conflicts than Holiday dinners (Barely using any now).

Comb your hair out straight after shampooing with cheap, generic stuff; no need to use conditioner (Followed whole life); style, let air dry; never use a blow dryer (Only done twice).

Detain from gambling any of your hard-earned cash as you will lose it (Burning it may be more fun; nah, save or invest it instead).

*E*at a bit of dark and white chocolate each day for balance and never feel guilty doing so (Yum!)

*F*inish every task you promise to do for everyone; just when you think one wee task you skipped was forgotten or unnecessary, boom (Only ever missed 2 big ones, and regret both).

*G*ifts don't require even a "Thank You"; otherwise they are not truly gifts (Secret Santa 24/7/365.25).

*H*old onto true friends, such as one who would call you at 3 am on a weeknight a few of weeks after your dear wife's passing to tell you he knows you're awake; is bringing pizza and beer over to your condo in 15 minutes; arrives, drinks, eats, chats about everything else except your loss; and leaves leaving you the leftovers (Thanks, MB!).

*I*ntolerate hypocrisy and ignorance; they are undiagnosed cancers (Learn, think, and reason).

*J*ump in to help anyone and everyone in need without asking or hesitating (Your generosity will be returned many-fold by strangers).

*K*eep your vote/no-vote to yourself in every election and forever (Done faithfully).

*L*earn something, anything, every day, then be able to state it out loud (Know more knowledge).

*M*arry, if you wish to and/or if your beliefs for faith requires, but make love rule in all partnerships (Hate simply does not compute, because everyone loses).

*N*ever give up no matter how long the odds or dark the situation (There is always hope).

*O*pen your heart and laugh, live, and love again even if your heart has been crushed (First-hand experience and practice).

*P*lease, no more bombing and wars; Gunky wants to retire (Peace means getting no bang for your buck).

*Q*uestion everything, but allow yourself to trust sometimes (Don't double-cross every bridge).

*R*eferee soccer matches for relaxation because its conflicts can put life's issues into perspective (Was in this alternative universe that Gunky's sanity was maintained; well sort of).

*S*porting tassels on your shoes will not make you more important if you do not deserve to be (Never worn; never will).

*T*ime is precious (As dear friend Dante shared, "You are dead a long time.").

*U*se your hands to wash and rinse dishes (Dr. Gunky's summer jobs were at a resort hotel as hand-dish washer, followed by grave digger for the poor and their pets using a shovel and a strong back; and then toilet-bowl cleaner to help Mom Gunky as a chamber maid; besides, dishwashers make great extra cupboard space in the kitchen).

*V*arnish your commentary with sarcasm if need be to help others listen, hear, and understand your conversation (Gunky was always accused of being way too sarcastic; so you think he cared? Yes, dammit!).

*W*ash your face with cool water by rubbing it with your hands; never use soap or a rag (Always did) and wash your clothes in cold water and only as really necessary have them dry-cleaned (Rarely did).

X always marks the spot where you are spinning on this Earth at 1037 miles per hour; hang on and enjoy the wild ride as long as you can; good luck (Gunky certainly has and plans too).

*Y*ou are only as good as your last bad decision or deed (What you decided or done wrongly lately should be a call to change).

*Z*ero in on the answer to the question you were just asked, and not the question you have in your mind, the answer to which has no relation to the information sought (A lost art, but those who can do this will be our future leaders).

If you are wondering, Gunky is currently conquering the stress of retirement. After all, it takes away your holidays, vacation, and weekends! Although it's starting to give him grey hair and wrinkles, he plans on taking deep breaths and being in every moment.

Speciousity (Bob are Words)

What it is.
It is not what.
It is a hole.
It is a spot.
Is it clear with an opaque hue?
Think for yourself.
What thinks for you?
Do as you are told.
What will not tell?
Just do your best.
But just do it well.

You know, when, like people, ah, mumble, um talk at Gunky, they basically, ah, like talk, um, like in sentences with, um, like, basically, with words. Really, actually?

This sad state of diction among the masses today was never "Bob's Way" of conversing. He had an efficient, albeit unconventional filler, a 2-word leading question. As be told, Bob was special in more ways than you could ever imagine. Here goes?

Gunky's lifelong friendship with Bob began with a handshake during which there was one-full and one-half smile exchanged, and one word, "Hi." Both had been invited to the 6th floor faculty-student lounge for a

10 am meet-and-greet their first day of graduate-school chemistry. Gunky was a PhD candidate; Bob a post-doc. With only 2 chairs left next to each other in the room, Bob sat opposite Gunky at the only open table in the corner. Like kismet?

Gunky asked Bob about his research and what he heard would be the first of many less-than-4-word answers, which would become Bob's hallmark. "Colored lasers." When asked what type of lasers, Bob said, "Bright ones." Gunky quickly picked up that Bob was shy and not much of a conversationalist. He'd never change. Like understatement? (OK; I'll stop with the likes).

After their first conversation, if you can call it that, both went about their work in below-ground labs, with Gunky's above Bob's. Their geolocation within the tower will become important to remember later. Both would see each other often coming at 6 am and going at 6 pm. Their only interaction was a wave, always initiated by Gunky, followed by, "Hi, Bob", which sometimes was returned with a slight grin. Brief encounter?

About 2 weeks later, Bob surprised Gunky by stopping by his lab one Monday morning shortly before 10 am. "Drink coffee?" Gunky said "Yes", and asked why he wanted to know, "Faculty lounge?" Gunky did not reply, but simply followed Bob down the hall to the elevator. Seven floors up, they entered the lounge where they first met. Bob poured a cup of black coffee while Gunky made iced coffee. While preparing his special brew, Gunky noticed Bob sit in the same chair at the same table where they had their inaugural chat. First reunion?

Joining him, Gunky asked Bob how he was doing with his experiments. "Don't know." Gunky then began what would become the tradition of carrying on a conversation with Bob by asking leading questions. Bob might start a chit-chat with a pair of unexplained words to which Gunky would always have to ask follow-up questions to keep going. Enough said?

His arrival at Gunky's lab door would repeat at 3 pm that memorable Monday, and continue twice-a-day almost every weekday for nearly two years. Coffee time?

Although few words ever came from of his mouth, there was plenty of activity inside his head. Bob understood the science of making light more brilliantly than anyone has or may ever will. Gunky once jokingly accused his close friend of being an alien and got a grin. Shiny objects?

Although succinct, Bob did have a flair for the dramatic. The first of his antics began with a rare phone call from him near 6 pm one Friday afternoon. The conversation went as follows; you will know who is speaking by virtue of the number of words in the sentence. Phone chat?

"Hello."

"Back wall."

"OK, what about my back wall?"

"Just watch."

"Which one is my back wall?"

"Silly question."

"OK, so what am I to see looking at what I think is my back wall?"

"Here comes."

"Whoa, you're shining a red dot on my wall!"

"Easy."

"How are you doing this?"

"Mirrors."

"OK, so you're using mirrors to shine a red dot on my wall from your lab downstairs?"

"Out, up, right." (Whoa! Bob just spoke a 3-word sentence!)

"What about any students walking down the hall; could they be blinded?"

"Crime-scene tape." (Double whoa! Two 3-word sentences in-a-row!)

"OK, you've impressed me, now what?"

"More power."

"OK, more power for what?"

"Brighter dot."

"Whoa! Has anyone else ever made laser-light so bright?"

"Don't know."

"OK, the red dot just got bri... Holy crap, the wall just caught fire!"

"Neat, huh?"

Gunky didn't hear Bob's soon-to-become-notorious 2-word last question because he had already thrown down the phone to grab a fire extinguisher. Gunky sprayed the wall just in time to stop the smoke detectors from sounding. He then turned on all hood vents to maximum. Relieved that Bob's first attempt at arson was stymied, Gunky returned to the phone. Chew out?

"Bob, just what in the Hell do you think you're doing?"

"Making bright light." (Whispered with a hint of amusement.)

"Pissed?" (Wow! Two sentences in-a-row from Bob for the first time!)

"Bob, this could get you kicked out of school!"

"No way."

"Yes, Bob, way!"

"Click". (Apparently Bob had run out of words!)

It took a while for Gunky to calm himself. This type of behavior from Bob came at a complete surprise. Gunky then realized that he had to expect the unexpected. Bobby trap?

Gunky's first thought was to go down to Bob's lab to give him a piece of his mind, but stayed in place to explain to anyone smelling smoke and coming by to find out what happened. Fortunately, no one seemed to notice; after all, this was a flame lab in a chemistry tower. Out damned spot? (Gunky's first 3-worder).

Monday morning rolled around and like clockwork Bob arrived at Gunky's lab and stood in the doorway. "Coffee?" Staring at the wall with his half-grin, he said, "My treat." How could you not like this epigrammatic genius thought Gunky? "You pay?"

Gunky covered the burn mark on the wall with a photo of Steinmetz, the Wizard of Schenectady, with his buddy Al (Einstein), the Wizard (of the World). Not one word was shared over coffee that morning because Gunky did not ask Bob any questions. Silent treatment?

There are many dangers inherent to working in chemistry-research labs. Safety is paramount and cowboys and corner-cutting are forbidden. It was just after 11 am when Gunky finished a flame test and was sitting at his desk looking at tons of data to analyze. Taking in a deep breath, he gagged on the smell of fish. He then took in a bigger whiff of the ocean breeze. Eyes watering, he realized this was a chemical release, and jumped up to turn the hood vents to maximum. Vacate premises?

As the odor seemed to disappear, he remembered Bob's last three pairs of double words at their 10 am coffee, "Big test; dark room; locked in". Gunky realized this meant Bob had isolated himself in his lab downstairs, oblivious to everything (more than usual). Gunky picked up the phone and called down to Bob. No answer. Gunky knew this meant trouble. How's Bob?

Bounding down the hall then stairs to Bob's lab he caught only a slight whiff of fish. His lab door was locked. Using the key Bob had given him, Gunky busted in calling out his name. No answer. Gunky then went into his laser lab. The fishy smell was overwhelming. He expected the worst and found it. Bob was slumped over in his chair as if napping. Shaking him, Bob stirred as if drunk. "Gotta get you outta here!" With Bob on his shoulder, Gunky dragged his chatty friend out the nearest emergency door, which opened to the loading dock. Fresh air?

Sirens! Someone had pulled the alarm and reported a chemical emergency; good move! When the response squads arrived, they gave Bob oxygen and loaded him up for hospital. Gunky was not allowed to ride in the ambulance as he wasn't related. Close call?

Bob's exposure to the chemical released was not life-threatening. All it did was make him very groggy and nauseous. Bob had several technicolor yawns on the way to hospital where was held overnight for observation. Bumpy tummy?

Turns out a careless grad student on the 10th floor had dumped the smelly liquid down the drain. This irresponsibility would have gone unnoticed had the elbows in floor drains in Bob's and Gunky's basement labs not dried out from lack of use. This emptiness allowed vapors to float directly from holding ponds beneath the building into their labs. Future exposure was prevented by periodically priming the drains, which Bob and Gunky faithfully did thereafter. Watering cans?

When retold by others, the story evolved into Gunky's saving Bob's life that day. Gunky didn't quite see it that way. However, from then forward Bob would talk to almost no one else except Gunky. Silent partner?

At following coffee breaks twice-a-day, Gunky began to know Bob better in baby steps, that is, 1, 2, 3, or 4-words at-a-time. Piece meal?

Then came the encore of the original enlightening performance. Do over?

"Hi, Bob."
"Back wall."
"Hey, not again!"
"Just watch."
"OK, what am I supposed to see this time?"
"Here comes."
"Big deal, you're shining a red dot on my wall again."
"Not done."
"Do I need my fire extinguisher?"
"Watch this."

"Whoa, the red dot just switched to yellow?"

"Again."

"Whoa again! It just changed to green?"

"More power."

"Don't you dare light my wall on fire again!"

"Got ya!"

This conversation was historic for two reasons. Comedic science?

First, on a personal basis, it was the first of the very few jokes Bob ever played on Gunky short of vandalism. Ha, ha?

Second, on a scholarly basis, what Bob did with his laser was cutting edge. Until then, no one had ever reported changing the brightness, color and power of a laser. His illuminating accomplishments resulted in his getting an immediate offer to work in a major Government lab to further develop his techniques. He would accept that job; be given a whiz-bang lab and handsome wage; and enjoy the next 30 years doing marvelous light tricks. Bye, Bob?

As years passed, annual calls around the Holidays between Bob and Gunky became less frequent. Although sometimes Bob called, it was always up to Gunky to sustain conversation by asking a series of leading questions. The most ironic words ever spoken by Bob were in response to a question on what he was researching, obviously classified. "Can't talk?"

Years later came an extraordinary call. Bob had not gotten any more verbose. Short, sweet?

"Hello."

"Hey, Bob, how are you doing?"

"Need tie."

"What, you don't have a tie?"

"You do."

"So you're saying you want one of my ties?"

"Mail it."

"What, you want me to mail you a tie across the country?"

"Home address."

"Don't they sell ties in your southwestern city?"

"No time."

"You mean it'd be faster for me to mail you one of my ties then for you to go buy one?"

"Regular mail."

"OK, prefer any color?"

"You chose."

"OK, I'll send you my best tie; I have 3 in my wardrobe."

"Send it."

"OK, I'll go home and mail it today."

"Tie tack?"

"Why do you need a tie tack?"

"Some event."

"What kind of event?"

"Some curly-haired dude." (Historic first 4-worder!)

"You're going to meet some young dude?"

"Short, too."

"You know this guy?"

"Gotta go."

"OK, Bob, the tie is in the mail."

"Bye."

A few weeks passed with no follow-up from Bob. So bizarre an episode, Gunky wondered if it had even occurred at all, then sort of forgot about it. Tie dream?

One day there was commotion in the faculty-student lounge. Gunky did go there on occasion, post-Bob. The excitement involved a news bulletin about Bob and his technical achievements, for which he was given a Distinguished Service Award. It had a photo that was most telling (pun intended!), because it showed Bob standing next to a short, curly-haired dude. Yes, you guessed it. Bob was wearing the very tie (sans tack) Gunky had mailed to him. What you might have not guessed was that the dude was a 2-Star General. Bob was half-grinning and holding a rather impressive plaque. High honor?

Gunky felt compelled to give call Bob that day. Catch up?

"Hey Bob!"

"Hi."

"Saw you won a big-time award for your laser work."

"No biggie."

"You mean a whopper of a plaque from a Major General isn't cool?"

"Short, curly-haired dude." (2nd of only six 4-word sentences ever!)

"Well, that award was very impressive."
"Dumped it."
"Say again."
"Trashed it."
"What do you mean you trashed it?"
"Wastepaper can."
"You threw away the plaque!"
"Tie too."
"What, you're telling me you threw away the plaque and my tie!"
"Not needed."
"What do mean you didn't need them."
"Stupid stuff."
"You may think they're stupid but someone doesn't!"
"Silly junk."
"Well thank you very much; that was my best tie."
"Not bad."
"You don't own a tie but you rate them?"
"All look alike."
"Well, I have to say Bob, you really did a number on us."
"Neat, huh?"
"Argh!"

Bob was not a total science nerd. In one of his last calls, he shared some scrabble about another way he had fun, which, again, had to be pieced together like a jigsaw puzzle. Straight shooter?

"Hi."
"Hey, Bob, it's been a while; what have you been up to?"
"Shot myself."
"What! How did you do that?"
"Gun, silly!"
"Duh, may I also assume it was loaded?"
"Live rounds."
"Didn't think a dummy round could shoot you."
"No, dummy."
"Were you in a duel?"
"On vacation."
"Were you on a murder-mystery cruise?"

"On horseback."
"Did your horse get you shot; did you steal it?"
"Spooked."
"I give up, Bob; what were you doing?"
"Rattlesnake hunting."
"So a rattlesnake shot you?"
"Ricochet, goofy."
"Did you live?"
"Snake did."
"Where were you when this happened?"
"Canyon."
"Think I got it now. A rock shot you?"
"Flesh wound."
"Where did you get hit?"
"Thigh."
"When did this happen?"
"Yesterday."
"Did you go to the hospital?"
"Stitched myself."
"Did you wear gloves?"
"Bear hands."
"Reported?"
"Just you."
"Bye."

Bob retired soon thereafter. To the angst of many, he disappeared like a hole in the water.

Gunky was called by Bob's handlers requesting information as to his whereabouts. Gunky claimed he knew nothing, which was very close to the truth. "But you were his best friend who told you everything." Gunky just grinned and thought to himself, Steinmetz and Einstein?

If you are wondering if Gunky knows where Bob is now, "Coffee break?"

Taming of the Screw (One Bad Turn Deserves...)

Was that an assault you did just witness?
This screwy adventure will tell.
Attempted impalement or near-miss?
Point is a stab would have been despicable!

It's the silly little things in life that matter most.

Growing up dirt poor, Gunky's family could rarely afford to give gifts for birthdays or holidays. Instead, all made valiant efforts to gather at home base; share a modest meal, giving thanks for the food, which at times was scarce; and engage in engaging conversation. No pity necessary readers, because despite their austerity, Gunky and his family were happy. Why? They were unaware they were poor. If they had been, they wouldn't have cared anyway. Most importantly, they were immune to the prevailing neurosis of gratuitous gift-giving. Their gift was Love.

On very special occasions, Gunky's Mom and Pop did give gifts, which, to some, might appear as trinkets. That would be a grand mistake, because they were treasures. There's one Gunky cherishes most. The year he was born, his parents had their first Christmas tree, cut down for free from similar woods where he had his close encounters, and potted it in a bucket of anthracite coal from their basement gallery. Every year thereafter, Pop would retrieve the same bucket of same coal; shove in a freshly cut evergreen; water daily; then enjoy. As a graduation gift, they picked out a lump of coal and attached a handwritten note saying, "Watered for 2 weeks every year the last 29." Gunky winked at this gem as he was writing this story. Precious!

This prelude was provided to give perspective to the next tale, which began as follows.

"Say what? Gunky grabbed his best-buddy's butt and shoved him out of the chair onto the ground? Are you saying Gunky just saved him from a fate-worse-than-death?"

This was the news flash over a decade ago late one warm summer eve on a plaza outside a college dorm. Its occurrence is commemorated in cities all around the globe even today in the form of holding another inanimate trinket-transformed-into-treasure.

Gunky's "Special Friend" stows away in its own petite, private, plastic pouch in his pocket awaiting paparazzi and pals. It goes viral.

The perpetrator was a rather ubiquitous object used not as intended, but as a "Weapon of Ass" destruction. Specifically, t'was a 2½-inch long steel screw stuck in-between the slats of a wooden outdoor bench. It had been purposely placed to painfully poke a portal into a person's patootie in a brutish backbiting manner. Wickedly cruel!

The random human target of this near-hit trembled as he told his colleagues of an attempt on his life. All listened intensely and quietly, butt with some disbelief, as he, too, was known as a storyteller. Everyone waited for the punchline, butt none came. They did not know whether he was joking or that it might have happened. At this point Gunky arrived. When everyone stared at him, he stared back, asking, "What?" Silence. He then reached into his pocket and premiered what would forever be known as "Mr. Screw". At that point, all became believers. Most thought it would have been too nonsensical to be otherwise.

About 3 months later, this same cast of characters was meeting again. After exchanging pleasantries about families, the survivor of the attempted stabbing stared at Gunky asking, "Well, did you bring it?" Gunky tried to look surprised and replied, "What?" Silence. When he put his hand into his pocket, his friend shouted, "No, you didn't!" Mr. Screw then made its encore to the roar of all. To commemorate the continuation of this happily-ended reunion, a photo was taken of the intended recipient holding his trophy. All this occurred in a pub in Montana before beers were ordered.

A similar cameo photoshoot would be repeated meeting-after-meeting for years around the country until a new tradition began, guest appearances. Gunky appointed himself guardian and official photographer, because he had an ulterior motive, difficult to keep clandestine.

To date, 27 folks have been snapped with Mr. Screw in 16 cities and 12 states. Special non-human celebrities photobombing have included a killer whale (orca mascot of the now-retired killer whale); a shark (color cartoon); a stingray (the car); and a four-story high, 72-foot-long skeleton (Brachiosaurus).

Locations have ranged from Arizona-to-New York and Montana-to-Texas; on water (San Francisco Bay) or near water (Niagara Falls); and in airports, banquet halls, baseball parks, and delicatessens. Mr. Screw did not require nor receive any makeup in any of the almost 50 photos, although many of Gunky's friends could have used some.

If you are wondering what effect growing up poor had on Gunky, know well that he will forever cherish the aesthetic gifts he was given, namely, the love of his parents and smiles from many dear friends holing a rusty screw. Think you'll get the point (no apology for this pun).

Under Your Sole
(Passing Thru)

One-o, two-o, three-o, five-o.
What bores thru rock giving it airflow?
Mole-e, hole-e on the ground amuck.
Spot-em, collect-em, and you'll be in luck!

    Gunky has an adult hobby so unusual that literally no words are available to describe it (come on now, it's not what you think!). Read on and you may agree it's actually holy. The only un-whole-some bit of this tale will be the solid put-down Gunky received from another notable writer. Get ready to disambiguate! Gunky's alphabet adventures are about to go-a-rocking.

    Gunky's hobby began serendipitously late one afternoon during one of his many strolls near water, this time on a Left Coast beach. Something odd caught his eye on the shore. He picked it up and was curious about how in the World a certain section of it could have been removed.

    Holding the light-grey, golf-ball-sized stone toward the setting Sun, he saw an orange dot from not 1 but 3 different holes. Closer scrutiny revealed these ins-and-outs were not the same size and offset, features suggesting they were not be manmade. To this day, Gunky has never confirmed how these penetrations were produced, nor does it matter. He penciled the date and location on the back of his first find, pocketed it, and carried-on.

About a year later roaming a Right Coast beach, he was admiring the curvature of the horizon while casually glancing down. After a couple of false alarms, he found a second, this one similar in size but dark grey and having only 1-hole. "Wow! They're all over!" But after about an hour of staring downwards, Gunky concluded that finding a companion was a hollow effort.

Couple of years later, Gunky was wandering the edge of one of the Great Lakes. Because the purpose a vacation is to do little or nothing, but do it well, he was again eyeballing the shore. You guessed it! Within minutes he found what became his Best of Show, a tan-colored 5-holer! Further searching yielded no joy, not disappointing because in his pocket was a real treasure.

Odd was his luck on walkabouts on the Gulf and Atlantic Coasts. Even was the hollowness near the Rio Grande, where the 2, 4, and 6-holers for his collection were filled in.

Gunky soon became eager to share his joy of collecting such novelties, but was between a...(you know the rest). How do you describe his hobby? Pet Rock® was already taken.

Being stumped, Gunky typed a letter to the man billed as the most famous etymologist of his times, whose gem of a last name fit the newspaper in which he work was print. Gunky's question to him, "What would you call someone who collects rocks with holes in them? To qualify, the holes must appear to have been made by some natural, albeit (word intentionally used to show off his vocabulary) unknown, process to penetrate through the rock."

To be clever, he proposed a hierarchy for collectors. Novices possessed 1-holers; Masters 2-holers; Grand Masters 3-holers; and Supreme Grand Masters those lucky enough to find a beauty with more than 3 holes. He then proudly proclaimed his capture of 6 such objets d'art, declaring himself as the World's 1st Super Supreme Grand Master. He ended his inquiry with the three words he thought most-aptly described his triumph, Im-Pres-*Sieve*.

The rocky ending alluded to in the intro will now be filled in, namely, the aforementioned snub. "I'm sorry, but I just don't have the time to research your query now. If and when the topic becomes topical, I'll do my best to deal with it in the column. Thanks for writing. Good luck in your quest. Sincerely, Willy Corundum."

It would have been sad enough if this empty response had arrived in a typed white form letter. Worse, it came on a preprinted light-blue form postcard! At least 15¢ was spent for the stamp!

After procrastinating for years to do so, Gunky learned from Electron University that hard-core collectors call their artifacts Lucky Stones. Now in retirement, Gunky spends about an hour a month looking for more of these gems. His collection now numbers over 200, with about 10% having more than one, with 6 of them more than 4 holes. No, Gunky's head does not have one.

If you are wondering why Gunky sometimes slowly strolls along head down, don't fret; he's not sad, but just trying to Rock on!

Virus, Your Forever Classmate (I Sneeze You)

There once was a one-time sneeze.
That exiled a class photo for sleaze.
Silly because how easy it was
To spoof, but cover your mouth please.

On the 1st day of his 6th and (almost) last-paying job, Gunky was having lunch with new colleagues, all of whom remain lifelong friends. They were a mix of young and old veterans and rookies, with no one was as green as Gunky. A curious bunch of highly-degreed scientists and engineers, notably one. To say this man was as brilliant as he was eccentric would be complimentary. Seems his mind was exceptionally preoccupied with staying healthy.

Gunky decided to eat a salad; loaded his bowl with just about every green thing from the bar; then returned to the table where his new mates were waiting. No sooner than he sat down when the person-of-interest offered the following warning, "You know, bean sprouts kill brain cells." Silence followed, although there were some bloated cheeks trying to swallow their laughter. Gunky struggled to think of something appropriate to say back. All he could come up with was, "OK, I'll say goodbye to my last two."

His colleague's obsession with threats against his health can be illustrated by how he had instrumented his office. The narrow strips of toilet paper hanging from the ceiling were not for decoration. They were strategically placed to make sure the air within the room was being properly circulated. Seems even his own breath was not healthy enough for him.

One day Gunky went to the auditorium to get his annual flu shot. Guess who was first in line? Odd about the scene was that his friend was carrying a very large and heavy book. After Gunky got his shot (he was No. 32), he saw his friend sitting at a table chatting with other colleagues. Gunky sat with them and could not resist asking about the book. "Why bring a book to read when you came early?" Nonchalantly he replied, "I'm studying the plausible, possible, and probable side effects of getting a flu shot while exercising my arm to make the vaccine flow more turbulently within it." He half-grinned when Gunky kidded him that, "If you bulk-up those guns any more we'll have to call you Mr. Fluniverse." He was a good sport.

To consummate proof of his paranoia, we must return 2-decades to his senior year in high school. He introduced his predicament to the group with the following, now infamous query, "Does anyone know of a clear and cogent monograph on the lifetime of a virus?"

Although not far from the oddball questions he typically posed, everyone stopped eating in amazement, waiting for an answer.

Gunky was the only one with courage to take the bait. "Well, speaking for myself, I don't know of any titles off-hand because bio-snot is not my subject matter expertise. Would you care to share why you need such medical data?"

Everyone at the table quickly chewed and swallowed the food in their mouths in anticipation of his answer. "Well, the day I received my senior yearbook, I looked at my photo and sneezed onto the page. I have never opened that book since, because I am not certain how long the virus smeared onto the page would live. Even though it's been over 20 years, I wouldn't want to get ill the same way again. Besides, I know what I look like."

If you are wondering, following his retirement celebration, Gunky's buddy admitted to not being overly preoccupied about his health and that he had been putting everyone on all along to justify his taking off as many sick days as possible. We told him we all knew this all along. Gesundheit!

Wanna Switch?
(Could be Worse)

We negotiate on spider web tightropes
Wobbling in the unstable state-of-living.
Striving to keep emotions in balance
And remain composed and forgiving.

So, do ya think you're havin a bad, bad day, do ya? So what happened to ya?

Did you get a wee paper cut or break a nail filing a document you had in electronic form, but couldn't find on your laptop desktop because it was too cluttered with cat-joke websites?

Did you get so overwhelmed texting about where to go for dinner representative of some strange country and thereafter shop and miss the opening pose in your Hatha yoga class?

Did you just want to scream when a daydreaming barista forgot 1 of the 7 qualifiers for your Tuesday morning multi-dollar cup of some liquid remotely resembling coffee, which he then refused comp?

Did you watch horrified as a bored landscaper rev-up a turbo-powered hedge trimmer and mutilate your prized, albeit inexpensive, 8-year old boxwoods, which were never meant to be pruned so they would keep their stunningly spherical shape?

Did you devote 2 years of your life conceiving a brilliant game-changing idea; win a patent for it; and be confident of being awarded a

$2-million proof-of-concept contract, which would earn you a promotion and job security, only to have the proposal miss the deadline by 6 minutes and be disqualified (non-protestable), because an admin failed to sign the disclosure page because of being preoccupied by shopping on-line for plastic toothpick holders in the shape of pink turtles?

Did you share this last calamity at dinner that night with your wife of over 30 years, who had declined eating after her last chemo and gently removed her wig nicknamed "Fluffy" to expose her bald, pale scalp to ask poignantly, "Want to trade places?"

If you are wondering, Gunky was at Peace at dinner that night and thereafter, thankful for realizing the answer to "What is important in life?" is in the question. Peace, love, play on.

Xtraordinaire
(Silent Sentinels)

Ever stoic, standing sturdy,
Enduring centuries of storm.
Guardians of civil beauty
Highlighting the horizon form.
Outlasting intermittent forces
From loud nocturnal flashes.
Singing seasonal choruses
To sooth between crashes.
Adapting to ambient changes,
Reinventing colors and shapes,
Surviving external invasions, then
Transforming into luxuriant landscapes.
Everywhere; ever there; ever free.

Dearest Winter

Infinite is my fascination
Of leafless one's imagination.
With masterpiece rainbow of colors brown
And circular intricacy up and down.
No matter the brightness of day or night
My heart races seeing their silhouette slight.

Arbor Again

Spider web branches radiate in random rows.
Patient nascence buds into sparkling glows.
Brilliant verdant passion erupts when each one knows.
Joyous annual curtain call to chromatic brown shows.

Summer Senses

Simmering green canopies swaying without a breeze.
Producing soft murmurs surely to please.
Restful slow-motions that jigsaw and tease.
Sightful, songful, sea-like sentries.

Fall Fiat

Spectral explosions announce imminent change.
Dotting their tops with chameleon-like range.
Then fanciful flight when wood's leaves estrange.
Nature's poly and monochrome beauty rearrange.

If you are wondering, Gunky can see the trees for the forest.

You'll Do (Double Tap)

For worse and better
We kept it together
And drove it home
With one headlight.

It was a cold, dark, and snowy Thursday December night, and all Gunky wanted to partake in was a Study Hour. You know, that time allotted during the week at college when you crack a book. It was not to be confused with Happy Hour, the 23 other ones devoted to drinking beer, playing cards, and watching tube.

Gunky's fraternity would make the one portrayed in "Animal House" look like a monastery. The day Gunky brought his parents to an open house is certainly representative. A Brother yelled, "Make a hole!" so another could drive his motorcycle down the spiral staircase with a young lady on the back riding topless. Pop said, "Tanned"; Mom said, "Oh my, she's not wearing a helmet!"

Gunky had secluded himself in his room. He had a physics final the next morning and thought it would be wise to at least find his textbook. He was in stealth mode because he had heard that The Sorority had invited his fraternity to an exclusive plenty o' beer, brats, and babes party. Despite this super-special big deal (3rd of its kind during the last 2 weeks), Gunky really needed and wanted to study physics, not physiques.

Near 8 pm, there was a commotion outside his door, through which burst 4 Brothers. They had his frat jacket in hand and soon Gunky in it and on their shoulders. "We will go together as one Brotherhood!", kidnapping Gunky and throwing his book into the trash can.

Twenty minutes later, all were in the local pub and dance hall. Gunky looked around and saw all his Brothers at the food table. "What is this, a cafeteria? If we're here, why don't we start dancing with this bevy of beauties?"

Squinting through the dimly lit, flashing disco floor, Gunky spied a somewhat tall foxy lady near the middle dancing with her coed friends and proclaimed, "I'm going in for the blond." He then made a wandering bee-line towards her. Unbeknownst to him, his roommate had heard his plan and bolted around the other side of the "herd" (warned you) toward the same target.

They arrived at almost the same time and each tapped on her nearest shoulder.

Which way would she turn and whom would she select? Gunky's destiny rested on her decision.

After glancing at each brother, she turned away from Gunky and started dancing with his roommate. "I'll be dipped!"

Spinning around, he saw a petite dark-haired coed for the first time and said to her, "You'll do."

Much to his surprise, she replied, "You'll do."

They danced, saying nothing to each other because the music was fabulously loud. When the band took a break after that song, they sat down together, including the blond and Gunky's roommate. Gunky and this little Russian woman then exchanged a series of wickedly clever personal insults. It was a match made in Long-Island/New-Jersey Heaven.

She said she didn't drink and that Gunky could have her cup of beer. After about half an hour of sarcastic quipping, Gunky asked on a flyer if she would go out with him the upcoming Saturday night. Her reply was a nonchalant, "No." She and her 5 suitemates then said they had to leave because their weeknight curfew was 11 pm, and it was a long hike back to their dorm, especially uphill in the snow. Bummer!

The blond with whom Gunky had intended to dance then asked, "Before we go back, could you please take a photo of us 6 girls?" Snap!

After they left, Gunky decided to go back to his frat room and study. Next day, he got a B on the final exam, best grade ever in physics. All that Saturday, he couldn't stop thinking about what a fun time he had had with her. In traditional manly fashion, however, he forgot her name.

Remembering names would be a problem plaguing Gunky the rest of his adult (?) life.

Sunday afternoon rolled around and almost all the frat boys were downstairs watching football. In its past life, the house was a funeral parlor and now housing 32 brothers with 1 phone.

When Gunky came downstairs, his Pledge Master said, "Gang of girls has been calling you all morning; 5 names are listed on the chalkboard by the phone. You're the popular guy! What you got going for you?" The room erupted in laughter. Gunky figured this was some kind of joke and didn't bother checking the board.

The phone rang several times over the next few hours, which other Brothers jumped to answer hoping the call was for them. Before going back upstairs to his room, Gunky did check out the names, which now filled the chalkboard. He recognized none, which convinced him it was all a joke. Then the phone rang again...

Because he was standing next to it, the Brotherhood insisted he answer it as the football game was in the first-15 of its last-2 exciting minutes. He did and it was for him. On the other end were her 5 coed roommates. Their request, please ask her out again because they liked Gunky better than the deadbeat she was dating. Gunky's reaction? He did not call her back and was satisfied with this decision because this must be Part-2 of an elaborately weird practical joke.

That winter was harsh, with feet of snow all around. Next Monday morning, Gunky walked up the long hill to campus planning to spend the entire day there. As usual, he got preoccupied in the science reading room; forgot the time; and missed dinner at the frat house, prepared by their beloved House Mother. What a grand woman! Took care of 32 jubilant, ah juvenile delinquents. The "Old Bat" was dating the town judge who always supported her boys. She and her pet dog were precious. But back to a pending assignation.

Because he needed food, Gunky departed from his normal return route. His meandering took him past the front of the Home Economics (remember that?) building. Gunky noticed the lights were on in only one room and that a single person was standing over a stove with an apron on looking out the window. Guess who? (From previous stories, you should know where this one is going, too!). Gunky gave her a casual wave. She returned her wave with an oven mitten.

About 10 pm, when the frat house phone first became available, Gunky decided to call her. One of her roommates answered; shrieked when she learned who it was; and said that they were waiting for Gunky's call. Her first word, "Hello?" with emphasis on the question mark.

All Gunky said was, "7 pm this Saturday night in the lecture hall lobby; movie?"

Her reply, "Paid last year to see the movie they're showing now for free, but, Yes."

If you believe these pick-up lines were ineffective, think again.

Three years later, including one entire summer apart, Petruskha and Gunky began their 36 years of marriage. The last 10 were the best. One Friday morning in the car on the way to countless chemo treatments she asked, "Where's my wig?" Gunky replied, "You mean Fluffy? It's in the back seat; I put a seatbelt on it to keep it safe." Her reply, "You haven't lost your charm, have you, dear? Love it."

The photo Gunky took the night they first met has December 3rd 1969 written on the back by her hand. Petruskha always teased Gunky that he kept this photo of the "Pretty Young Things", as they called themselves, because it included Blondie. It also had another timely item.

A few weeks after December 3rd, 2008, when she lost her valiant battle, Gunky started a scrapbook of all the photos of her and their children. That first photo absolutely positively stunned. Not because of Petruskha, or even Blondie, being in it, but because of the clock in the background that read 9:44 pm. Even before he checked her death certificate Gunky knew the significance of this time. These exact correspondences of date and time would be the first of many signs she would send Gunky demonstrating her courage, willpower, and everlasting love.

If you are wondering, yes, Gunky considers himself to be truly blessed.

Ziggity-Zaggity Blinkedy-Blink (Razzing Rubicundity)

They're dark and looming out there.
So evil but subliminally unclear.
There're dots and dashes as you stare.
Warning you to begin to take care.
I think it's time to wake up
Drivers, what's in your sight?
Something's planning some real fright.

Conspiracy lies deep.
Into your psyche it will seep.
Starts when you're driving your car.
Ends when you've gone not too far.
I think it's time to walk.
People, better take a hike.
Something's planning to invade alright.

Worried about genomic mutation by additives in your water; psychological manipulation by chemtrails in your skies; or thought-bending by radiation from cell-phone towers? Pish-posh!

Do you suspect (as Director-FBI confirmed) you are being watched and listened to by your television even when turned off? Poppy-cock!

Ever worry if we masses are being brainwashed by some malicious evil force, which, after a chosen moment, will switched on to control of all human will? Probable!

All seriousness aside, THEY are THE most-sinister THINGS ever unleased by THEM!

Cryptic demonic codes have been subliminally and ubiquitously programmed into the World's population for over a century. Even worse, more messages will be implanted into your psyche right before eyes in full display every next day and night no matter where you travel.

Although you have been staring right at them all along, you probably have not really seen them in their true light. Now is the time for Gunky to put his foot down and STOP to this!

If Gunky ever does anything in his life for the betterment of Humankind, it will be to give this alert and inform Planet Earth to the treachery lurking in these glowing entities. Heed This!

Silent signals shine in several silhouettes and sizes, serially shape-shifting into shimmering symbols. Small scarlet soldiers surface side-by-side in singular swarms and shine subsequent to a simple step.

So if you're wondering one last time (for now), wonder some more. Gunky knows what this menace is. Have you put your foot down on what it is? To be continued... BCNU.

"*Look for a sign, which you might not see right away. That will be me beaming my love to you, which will dry your tears, warm your heart, and comfort your soul. That's all Babe.*"

For Reason Must Prevail. Peace, Love, Play On!

CPSIA information can be obtained
at www.ICGtesting.com
Printed in the USA
LVHW111341050919
630045LV00001B/43/P

9 781489 723949